The Ghost
with
Blue Eyes

Also by Robert J. Randisi
in Large Print:

The Dead of Brooklyn
No Exit from Brooklyn

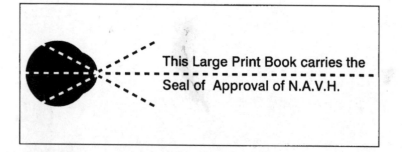

This Large Print Book carries the
Seal of Approval of N.A.V.H.

Robert J. Randisi

The Ghost with Blue Eyes

Thorndike Press • Waterville, Maine

Copyright © 1999 by Robert J. Randisi

Published in 2002 by arrangement with
Leisure Books, a division of Dorchester Publishing Co., Inc.

Thorndike Press Large Print Western Series.

The tree indicium is a trademark of Thorndike Press.

The text of this Large Print edition is unabridged.
Other aspects of the book may vary from the original edition.

Set in 16 pt. Plantin by Al Chase.

Printed in the United States on permanent paper.

Library of Congress Cataloging-in-Publication Data

Randisi, Robert J.
    The ghost with blue eyes / Robert J. Randisi.
        p. cm.
    ISBN 0-7862-4673-1 (lg. print : hc : alk. paper)
    1. Large type books.   I. Title.
PS3568.A53 G48 2002
813′.54—dc21   2002028563

To Marcus, my blue-eyed pseudo-son.

Prologue

Big Bend, Kansas — September 1883

When Lancaster stepped off the train onto the platform in Big Bend, Kansas, he looked both ways and saw no one else exiting the train. Farther down he could see his dun being off-loaded from the stock car. Apparently he was the only one with business in Big Bend that day. That suited him.

"Mr. Lancaster?"

He turned in the direction of the voice and saw a short, well-dressed man of about forty-five approaching him. The man was very slender and had a look of apprehension on his face that was not at all hidden by a heavy mustache.

"I'm Lancaster."

Lancaster wore a long duster over a heavy shirt and Levi's, and a flat-crowned black hat. Beneath the duster, on his right hip, he wore his weapon of choice, a .45 single-action Colt Peacemaker, nickel-plated with hard rubber grips. He had large hands, and he needed a large gun to fit.

It was very cold, and the other man came

close enough for their frosted breath to mingle.

"Are you Kane?" Lancaster asked.

"Uh, no," the man said, "but Mr. Kane sent me to meet you. My name is Carlyle."

Lancaster once again looked down toward the stock car. A man was holding the reins of his horse. It was not the same man who had walked the animal off the train. Lancaster looked at Kane's man, Carlyle.

"He works for Mr. Kane," the man said. "If it's all right with you, I'll signal him to take your horse to town?"

"Sure," Lancaster said. "Go ahead."

Carlyle waved his arm and the man holding the reins started away from the train, leading the horse. Lancaster heard the train start up and move away behind him.

"Where do we go?" he asked the other man.

"Uh, to town, also. Mr. Kane has arranged a room for you at the hotel."

"Who are you?"

"I told you, my name is —"

"I know your name," Lancaster said. "Who are you?"

"Oh, yes. I'm Mr. Kane's assistant."

"Is it Carlyle something," Lancaster

asked, "or something Carlyle?"

"Carlyle is my last name," the man said. "My first name is Henry."

"Well, Henry," Lancaster said, "lead on. I'm anxious to hear what it is Mr. Kane wants to hire me to do."

"Yes, well," Carlyle said nervously, "this way, then. Can I take your bag —"

Lancaster moved his hand away, the one with his carpetbag in it. His extra gun was in there — a big Walker Colt that was once his primary weapon — along with some clothes, and he never let anyone touch it.

"I'll take it. Just lead the way."

"Uh, yessir," Carlyle said. "It's, uh, this way."

They walked to the end of the platform where the ticket office was and stepped down. Lancaster followed Carlyle into the town of Big Bend, which did not quite live up to its name. It appeared to be a collection of ramshackle wooden structures, unevenly spaced and in need of repair.

"It's not much now," Carlyle said, as if reading Lancaster's mind, "but Mr. Kane intends to build it up."

"That'll take a lot of money, from the looks of things."

"Mr. Kane has a lot of money."

"Well," Lancaster said, almost smiling,

"I'm glad to hear that."

Carlyle put his hand to his mouth, as if he realized that he had said more than was necessary.

There were a few people on the street, and they tossed curious looks at Lancaster as he continued to follow Carlyle to — he assumed — the hotel.

"There's the hotel," Carlyle said, indicating a two-story building that was obviously a recent addition to the town. It was new, and solidly built. Above the door was a sign that said simply: HOTEL.

"We haven't thought of a suitable name for it yet," Carlyle commented.

"How about Kane House?"

"Mr. Kane is much too modest for that."

Lancaster had known a few men with lots of money, and none of them had ever been modest. He was interested in meeting Hannibal Kane.

As they crossed the street to the hotel they passed a woman and a little girl about six years old. Lancaster touched the brim of his hat and the woman looked away nervously. The child, however, stared up at him with complete fearlessness. Her eyes were the bluest he had ever seen, a shocking blue that dominated her face. They were filled with curiosity and an innocence that was completely alien to Lancaster. The woman grabbed the child's hand and pulled her along. Obviously, she intended to extinguish the innocence by teaching the child fear.

"Your room is on the second floor."

"Are we going there now?"

"I, uh, thought you'd like to get settled in before you saw Mr. Kane."

"You thought wrong, Henry," Lancaster said. "I'd like to see Mr. Kane first. If I don't take the job, there won't be any need for the hotel. I'll be on the next train."

"I see," Carlyle said. "Well, I suppose I could take you to Mr. Kane's office . . ."

"Why don't you do that."

"Yes, uh, well, it's this way, then."

Carlyle led Lancaster away from the hotel and deeper into town. There Lancaster saw another building that was a recent addition. This one was made of brick, standing two stories high and dominating the center of town.

"The large plate-glass window on the second floor," Carlyle said. "That's Mr. Kane's office."

As they got closer, Lancaster could read the writing on the window: KANE & ASSOCIATES.

"Who are the associates?"

11

"Mr. Kane has many," Carlyle said, "but he usually has controlling interest in whatever business endeavor he's involved in."

"That figures."

Lancaster followed Carlyle into the building and up to the second floor. They went through a door and into an office with a woman sitting at a desk. She was efficient looking, primly dressed, in her fifties. She looked up as the two men entered.

"Mr. Carlyle," she said.

"Mrs. Bailey," Carlyle said, "this is Mr. Lancaster to see Mr. Kane."

"Why didn't you take Mr. Lancaster to the hotel first?" she asked.

"He, uh, didn't want to go."

"I see."

"I'd like to see Mr. Kane as soon as possible," Lancaster said.

"Well, sir, Mr. Kane is very busy. If you would care to go to the hotel and get settled —"

"I *am* settled already, lady," Lancaster said, dropping his carpetbag to the floor. "I don't want to go to the hotel, I want to see Mr. Kane . . . now."

Without even moving, Lancaster, who stood an inch over six feet, suddenly seemed to loom over Mrs. Bailey.

"Yes, well," she said uneasily, sliding her

chair back, "I will let Mr. Kane know you are here."

"Thank you."

The silence between Lancaster and Carlyle in Mrs. Bailey's absence was awkward — for Carlyle. Lancaster was unaffected by it. Total silence was so rare for him, in fact, that he simply stood there and enjoyed it. For that reason Mrs. Bailey's return came too soon to suit him.

"You may go in," she said. "Mr. Kane will see you now."

Lancaster went through the open door without a further word to either Carlyle or Mrs. Bailey. He carried his bag with him.

"Mr. Lancaster, I'm so glad you're here." The man standing behind the desk — Hannibal Kane — was tall, white-haired, robust for a man obviously in his sixties. His complexion was almost pink, except for the red lines on his nose. It was obvious Mr. Kane liked to take a drink or two.

"Your offer of one thousand dollars just to talk was very persuasive, Mr. Kane."

"I thought it might be. Have a seat. Would you like a drink?"

"A small whiskey, if you have it," Lancaster said, sitting down, "to cut the dust." He put his bag down gently next to the chair.

Kane walked away from his huge, cherrywood desk to a side bar and said proudly, "I've got some very fine brandy. I'm sure you'll like it."

"Just a whiskey," Lancaster said.

Kane hesitated, then said, "Well, all right, then, a small whiskey it will be."

He poured a whiskey for Lancaster and a brandy for himself. He walked back behind his desk and put the whiskey down in front of Lancaster.

Lancaster picked up the whiskey, tossed it off, and set the glass back down.

"I'd like to get to the offer," he said. "The next train going back is in an hour, and I'd like to be on it if we don't make a deal."

"Oh, we'll make a deal, all right," Kane said. "Trust me on that."

"No offense," Lancaster said, "but there are only two men in the world I trust, and you're not one of them. What's this deal?"

"Very well," Kane said, putting his brandy down untouched, "we'll get right to it, then. I am willing to pay you ten thousand dollars to kill a man."

Lancaster hesitated just a moment — the amount mentioned was worth *that* — then picked up his bag and stood up.

"I'll be going, Mr. Kane," he said, and started for the door.

"What? Wait, I don't understand."

Lancaster stopped halfway to the door and turned to face the man again.

"I'm not a killer."

"But — but I understood that you hired out your gun."

"Yes, I do," Lancaster said, "but I don't hire out as a killer. I do work that sometimes requires me to use a gun."

"I'm afraid I don't see the difference."

"I'm really not concerned with whether you see the difference or not, Kane," Lancaster said. "All you need to know is that I am not a hired killer. Good day."

"But —"

Lancaster didn't wait to hear the "but."

Carlyle jumped to his feet when Lancaster came out of the office.

"Shall we go to the hotel now?" he asked.

"No," Lancaster said, "back to the train station."

"I beg your pardon?"

"I'm leaving on the next train. Your boss and I were not able to make a deal."

"But — but —" Carlyle stammered. He thought that Hannibal Kane had enough money to make a deal with anyone.

Kane appeared at the door and snapped at Carlyle.

15

"See Mr. Lancaster back to the train station, Henry."

"I can find my way," Lancaster said.

"Please," Kane said, somewhat stiffly, "at least let me supply you with an escort."

Lancaster looked at the man, then at Carlyle.

"All right, Henry," he said, "lead the way."

They were on the street only for a moment when there was a shot. Carlyle yelped and jerked at the same time, then slumped to the ground.

Lancaster turned quickly, his hand reaching beneath his duster for his pistol. He stopped when he saw the man pointing a gun at him.

The man holding the gun was tall and rangy. He held his pistol in his right hand, and it was pointed directly at Lancaster.

"You must be Kane's gunman," he said.

"Who are you?"

"Me? I'm your job."

Lancaster stared at the man.

"Didn't Kane tell you about me?"

"No."

"But you're here to take a job, right?"

"No," Lancaster said again.

"Well, I'm it," the man said. "My name's McCray, and you're being hired to kill me."

"No, I'm not," Lancaster said. "I don't hire out as a killer."

"Bull," McCray said. "I know your name, Lancaster. You have a rep as a man with a fast gun."

"Maybe so," Lancaster said, "but I don't have a reputation as a hired killer."

"It don't matter what you say," McCray said. "You and me are gonna settle this now."

Lancaster looked at the fallen man, unsure whether he was alive or dead. Then he looked at McCray.

"Do you want me to turn around, so you can backshoot me like you did him?"

McCray laughed.

"That was just to get your attention. I don't need to backshoot anyone."

"Then holster it," Lancaster said.

The man studied Lancaster for a few more moments, then shook his head and holstered his gun.

"Let's get to it, then," McCray said. "I've got things to do."

What transpired next seemed to Lancaster to happen in slow motion. McCray went for his gun, as did Lancaster. While McCray strove for speed, Lancaster was more deliberate. He may not have gotten his gun out as fast as most, but his first shot was

17

usually more accurate.

McCray snapped off a quick shot that punched a hole through Lancaster's duster but did not strike him. Lancaster fired, and his bullet struck McCray in the chest. With a shocked look on his face McCray fell to one knee. He struggled to bring his gun up again, and Lancaster fired a second time . . . and heard a woman's voice scream, "No!"

He didn't see the little girl until it was too late. McCray was on his knee, and Lancaster was standing on the boardwalk in front of the hotel. Consequently he was firing at a definite downward angle. It was for this reason that the bullet struck the little girl as she ran between the two men.

Just before she was struck, however, she turned and looked at Lancaster and he saw her blue eyes staring at him — and then the bullet struck her, extinguishing those eyes forever.

Seconds later he felt the hot lead strike him in the upper chest, on the left side, and he was falling over. . . .

Chapter One

When Lancaster woke he stared up at a cracked, yellowing ceiling. It took him a moment to collect his thoughts and recollect everything that had happened.

He heard voices that seemed to be coming from far away, perhaps outside. He turned his head and saw that he was in a room with two men.

"What —" he said, but nothing else came out. The one word, however, was sufficient to attract the attention of the two men. He saw that one of them was wearing a badge. The other was wearing a white coat, and Lancaster assumed he was a doctor.

"How do you feel?" the doctor asked.

He felt lousy. His shoulder hurt, and he said so.

"The bullet hit you high up, so there was no damage to the heart. You were lucky."

Lancaster wet his lips.

"McCray?"

"The other man? He's dead. He got one last shot off at you and then died."

Lancaster wet his lips again and spoke slowly.

"And the little girl?"

"Becky Pickens," the doctor said. "I'm sorry, she's dead."

Lancaster turned his head to look at the sheriff, but instead he saw the little girl standing there, staring at him with those startling blue eyes. . . .

Dunworthy, Texas — March 1884

"Jesus!" he shouted, and sat up.

He looked around him at the darkened room and realized that he'd had the dream once again. It was accurate except for the little girl replacing the sheriff. He *had* awakened in the doctor's office after the doctor had removed the bullet from his shoulder and bandaged him. He *had* looked over at the sheriff, at which time the man had ordered him to leave town. He *had* heard the murmur of voices from the mob outside that wanted to string him up for what happened to eight-year-old Becky Pickens. It didn't matter to them that it was an accident. If Lancaster had died and McCray had survived they would have wanted to hang him instead.

Lancaster looked around the dingy room and slowly remembered where he was, in a

small room behind the saloon in Dunworthy, Texas.

After leaving Big Bend, Kansas, he had traveled quite a bit from town to town, but he could not seem to outrun the dreams, in which the girl with the blue eyes visited him. She seemed like a blue-eyed ghost, following him wherever he went, until he finally sought refuge in the bottle — but the whiskey just seemed to make her visits more real.

He had gone to sleep fully dressed again, and was covered with sweat. He swung his feet to the floor and stood up from the pallet he used as a bed. He staggered to the back door and opened it, then staggered again as the sunlight struck his face. He leaned against the doorjamb for a moment, holding his hand up to shade his eyes from the sun, then stepped outside. He made his way to the horse trough, fell to his knees, and stuck his head in it. The water was stagnant and warm, but it washed away some of the cobwebs.

He pulled his head out of the trough and used both hands to brush his hair back. That done, he cupped some more water with his hands, rubbing his face and eyes vigorously.

He stood and then sat on the edge of the

trough. The water leaked from the point of his chin and pooled on the ground between his feet. He looked around at the area behind the saloon, then up at the sky. The sun was high, so he surmised it was nearly three in the afternoon. Had he gotten drunk the night before? Probably. The dream had seemed particularly vivid.

He had been in Dunworthy for three months now, working at the saloon as a swamper. The only thing that kept him from being the town drunk was that he did not get drunk every night. That honor belonged to Caleb Janeway. Old Caleb seemed to be drunk all the time, morning, noon, and night.

Lancaster knew he had sunk low, but he hadn't hit rock bottom yet. Maybe that was why he had chosen to stay in Dunworthy. As long as Caleb Janeway was at the bottom there would be no room for him.

He removed his shirt and bathed his chest and neck with the lukewarm water, then submerged his shirt and wrung it out. He put it on a nearby fence to dry. Did he have another? He couldn't remember.

He watched the water as it settled. When it was still and clear he could see his reflection, and then the reflection of something else, something with blue eyes. He turned

quickly, but he couldn't catch her. He never could . . . not that she was ever really there. He knew that. Still, seeing her like that was better than the times when she actually spoke to him. . . .

He stood up and walked back to the saloon, entering the back room again. He looked around to see if he had another shirt. He opened an old chest that the owner was letting him use in lieu of a dresser. He did indeed have another shirt, and as he took it out he saw his gun and gunbelt.

It had been six months since the shooting of the little girl. He'd traveled for three months, wearing the gun but not using it again. When he settled in Dunworthy he decided to take the gun off and put it away. It had been in that chest ever since.

He closed the chest on the gun and donned the shirt. It wasn't exactly clean, but at least he hadn't sweated through it during the night.

He left the room and went out into the saloon. Dunworthy was a small town, but a growing one. The saloon was busier at three in the afternoon on this day than it was when he first walked into it. Frank, the owner and bartender, said it would be even busier three months from now.

"Lancaster," somebody said by way of

greeting, and Lancaster just waved and kept going.

"Poor bastard," the man who'd greeted him said as he went by.

"He's a drunk," another man said.

There were three men sitting at a table, and the third man said, "I heard he was pretty good with a gun once. I wonder what happened?"

"He's a drunk," the second man said again.

"Yeah, but what made him a drunk?"

"Same thing makes anybody a drunk," the third man said. "He fell into a bottle one day and couldn't get out. Still can't."

"Can't be more than what? Thirty?" the first man said. It had been a long time since he'd seen thirty — or since any of the three of them had.

"He looks forty," the second man said. "That's what bein' a drunk does to ya."

"Still," the first man said, shaking his head, "it's a shame. . . ."

Lancaster got to the batwing doors of the saloon and stopped, staring outside.

"Hey, Lancaster!" Frank Keller yelled from behind the bar. He had been a handsome man most of his life, but as he got older he got heavier, until, middle-aged now, he tended bar because he thought it would hide his girth.

Lancaster turned and looked at him.

"Ya didn't sweep up this mornin'."

"I overslept."

"Yeah, well, ya do it again and you're fired, ya hear?" Frank shouted, not caring who heard.

"I hear," Lancaster said, and stepped outside, wondering how he'd gotten to this point in his life. Six months earlier he'd been fine, happy even, working, doing what he was good at, and then that damned little girl had to run between him and McCray.

It wasn't even that she had died. It was that, even dead, she wouldn't go away. It was that he always seemed to see those blue eyes, whether he was asleep or awake.

They were supposed to be closed forever. Goddammit, why wouldn't they close?

Chapter Two

Lancaster was still standing in front of the saloon when the stage came into town. The stage stop was right down the street, in front of the hotel. The driver reined his team in and applied the brake before dropping to the ground. He ran to open the door, and as Lancaster watched a man stepped out, then helped a pretty young woman step down. She was wearing a blue dress and a bonnet that shouted "easterner." She turned, reached into the stage with both hands, and lifted a little girl out and set her down on the ground. The girl was similarly dressed in a blue dress and bonnet, and appeared to be about eight or nine years old.

Lancaster felt a chill run through him as he looked at the woman and the child. Suddenly, the little girl turned her head and looked directly at Lancaster, and he saw that she had blue eyes — startling blue eyes.

He closed his eyes and rubbed them with the heels of both hands, then looked again, but by then the woman and child had entered the hotel. Was it his imagination that the girl had blue eyes?

He walked over to where the stage was sitting, empty now that its only passengers had disembarked. He turned away from it and walked to the front door of the hotel. From there he could see the woman and girl standing at the front desk, their backs to him. He stared at the girl, trying to will her to turn around and look at him again, but she never did. Her mother accepted a key from the desk clerk and they both went up the stairs.

Lancaster turned and walked slowly back to the saloon, still wondering if his mind was playing tricks on him. He was going to have to keep an eye out for that little girl. He had to get a closer look at her. . . .

Sheriff Dan Mathis watched as the stage pulled in, on time, as usual. He made it a point to be there when the stage arrived every day. He wanted to see who got off, where they went. It made it easier to find them and question them afterward. He saw a man get out, a well-dressed man in a black gambler's suit. He'd be questioning him very soon. Mathis didn't like slick gamblers coming into his town and fleecing the citizens.

The gambler reached into the stage to assist a pretty woman in a blue dress out of the coach. She in turn reached in, lifted out a little girl of about eight or nine, and set her on the ground.

Mathis watched long enough to determine that the woman and child were not with the man, they had simply traveled in the same stage. The woman seemed to thank him, and the gambler tipped his hat to both her and her little girl and then walked away. Not surprising that he headed for the saloon, which had several rooms to rent above it. That would put the man closer to the action.

The mother was more than attractive. Her hair was blond, and pinned up on her head to reveal a long graceful neck. Her traveling clothes flattered her figure, which was slender, yet full in the right places. Mathis wondered if she was a new girl for the saloon. If she was, she would sure bring some class to the place.

The woman and little girl went into the hotel, the stage driver coming up after them, carrying their luggage. Pretty women got that kind of treatment.

Mathis noticed something else. He saw Lancaster, the swamper at Frank Keller's saloon, watching the stage, and studying the woman and girl. The man even walked over to the hotel and stood in front of it, staring into the lobby. Guess the man wasn't too far gone to appreciate a pretty woman.

Couldn't be far from it, though, from what Mathis saw. A damned shame. Mathis knew Lancaster's reputation. Wouldn't be long, now that the man had taken off his gun, before somebody — probably somebody real young, full of piss and vinegar — would come along and kill Lancaster. Might even be the best thing to happen to the poor bastard.

Mathis stepped down off the boardwalk in front of his office and headed for the saloon. Might as well question that gambler sooner than later.

Upstairs in their hotel room Alicia Adams turned to her mother, Margaret, and asked, "Did you see that man, Mommy?"

"What man, honey?"

"The man who was looking at us?"

Margaret Adams turned to her little girl and smiled down at her.

"Honey, you're a very pretty little girl. You'll find that as you grow up and become a pretty woman men will look at you."

"Like you, Mommy?"

"Yes, honey, like me. The trick is not to

let them know that you know they're looking."

"Why not, Mommy?"

Margaret cupped her little girl's chin in her hand and said, "You'll find out, pumpkin."

"When, Mommy?"

"Soon, darling, very soon." Margaret hoped it wouldn't be too soon. "Let's get you out of that dirty dress now and into something pretty and clean."

"I'm hungry, Mommy."

"I know you are, dear. We'll eat as soon as we're changed."

Margaret Adams was very proud of the fact that her daughter looked like her. She knew what a pretty woman she was, because men had told her for years. She also knew that Alicia was going to be just as pretty, if not more so. She only wished that her daughter had inherited her hazel eyes instead of her father's brown ones.

Chapter Three

For the next week Lancaster took every opportunity to get a look at the little girl. It was evident that she and her mother were settling in Dunworthy. At the end of the week they were still staying in the hotel, and all Lancaster had to do to get a look at them was sit in front of the saloon.

Sometimes he followed them, usually when they went shopping. A time or two the little girl saw him and waved. He waved back, but they never spoke. All he knew from the first time he laid eyes on her was that he couldn't let anything happen to her. When he wasn't working in the saloon, he was watching the little girl, whether she was with her mother or not.

It soon became clear to him that the little girl's mother was the new schoolteacher, so she and her mother were usually in the schoolhouse at the same time. Once, when the children were outside playing, he had been sitting off to one side watching them. To his surprise, the little

31

girl walked right up and boldly spoke to him. The blue of her eyes made him wince.

"Hello," she said.

"Hi."

"I'm Alicia."

"Hi, Alicia."

"Why are you always watching us?" she asked. "Me and my mommy?"

It hadn't dawned on him that either of them had noticed him, but now that he thought about it, it made sense. He was, after all, not bothering to hide.

"To keep you safe."

"From my daddy?"

Lancaster frowned.

"Do you need to be kept safe from your daddy, Alicia?" he asked.

But before she could answer, her mother appeared in the doorway of the school-house. She called for all the children to come back inside, and when she saw Alicia standing in front of Lancaster she called especially loud for her daughter to return.

"I have to go," Alicia said. " 'Bye."

"Goodbye."

He watched as the little girl ran back to the schoolhouse, where her mother obviously gave her a tongue-lashing, probably about talking to strangers. Before closing

the door Margaret Adams gave Lancaster one last look.

Margaret Adams wasn't quite sure how long the man had been watching them. He couldn't have possibly recognized them, could he? Did he know who they were? Were they going to have to leave this town so soon?

She decided to talk to the sheriff that very day about the man, to see what she could find out.

"He's just the swamper in the saloon, ma'am," Sheriff Mathis said. "He's harmless, really."

"And has he lived here long?" She was seated in a chair across the desk from the lawman. Mathis couldn't believe how pretty she was up close. Pale skin, white teeth, red lips. He wished he had combed his hair, or put on a clean shirt this morning.

"About three months."

That was good. Nobody could have predicted three months ago that she would be in Dunworthy, Texas. Still, she didn't like the way the man followed them, the way he looked at Alicia.

"Sheriff, I wonder if you could speak to the man," she said. "Just tell him . . . just as

33

him not to follow us. . . . He's scaring my little girl."

"Don't you worry, Miss Adams," Mathis said. "I'll put a stop to it."

"I don't want you to . . . hurt him, or anything. Maybe just . . . scare him a little?"

"I'll take care of it, ma'am," Mathis said. "He won't bother you anymore."

"Thank you, Sheriff," she said. "That makes me feel a whole lot better."

At dinner that night Mathis spoke to his wife about the schoolteacher's complaint.

"Lancaster?" she asked. "Isn't he that man who works in the saloon?"

"That's right."

Cynthia Mathis set the last of the dinner bowls on the table, one with steaming mashed potatoes in it, then sat down across from her husband. Mathis had always counted himself lucky that Cynthia had married him twelve years before. She was a handsome woman — then and now. Could be, he thought often, she could have done better. Theirs was a childless marriage, but they both kept busy, and although they never seemed to have money his position as sheriff gave them a small house to live in while he was in office.

"He's harmless, isn't he, Dan?" she

34

asked. "Isn't that what you told me?"

"He seems to be," Mathis said. "At least, up until now."

"Didn't you say he had a violent background, though?"

"He had a rep with a gun for many years."

"Not too many years," she said. "Surely, he's not that old."

"Not at all," Mathis said, "but he took to the gun early, as I understand it."

She suddenly put her fork down and covered her mouth with both hands as she realized something.

"He's the man who had that horrible thing happen — where was it? Oklahoma?"

"Kansas."

Mathis had a habit of discussing the events of the day with his wife each evening at dinner, and he generally told her everything. When Lancaster had first come to town and Mathis had checked him out, he'd told her the whole story.

"That poor man — and this is a mother and little girl he's following?"

"Yes."

"It's the little girl, Dan."

"What is, darlin'?"

"He's watching the little girl."

"I know," Mathis said, "and I've got to get him to stop."

"The poor, poor man," she said, picking her fork up again.

"Great meat loaf, as usual, Cyn."

She nodded, hardly hearing him.

Chapter Four

Lancaster woke the next morning to someone pounding on the door of the back room.

"Wha—" he called.

"Lancaster? This is Sheriff Mathis. Get out here!"

"What the . . ." Lancaster said, putting his bare feet on the floor. He walked to the flimsy door and opened it. He was surprised that the sheriff's knocking hadn't torn the darn thing off.

Lancaster had met Dan Mathis briefly when he first came to town. It was the sheriff's job to check on strangers. Mathis kept an eye on him right up to when he got his job. From that point on, when Lancaster was no longer considered a transient, the lawman stopped paying special attention to him. They had crossed paths only occasionally since then.

Lancaster opened the door, and the sheriff glowered at him. Mathis was a big man and might have once been considered powerfully built, but now he was just . . . well, big. His face was round, and his belly — which hung over his belt — was, too.

"What's the matter, Sheriff?"

"Come out here and sit down," Mathis said. "I want to talk to you."

"What time is it?" Lancaster asked, rubbing his face.

"Never mind that."

"Let me get dressed —"

"You don't have to. Nobody's in the saloon yet."

"What?" Lancaster asked. "It's that early?"

"Don't make me ask you again."

There was a time no one would have spoken to Lancaster that way. He himself was a big man, an imposing figure once, but he had gone the opposite way of the sheriff. Instead of getting fat, Lancaster had gotten very thin, almost painfully so.

"I'm comin'," Lancaster said.

He came out of the room, walked to a table, and sat down, wondering what he had done to bring the sheriff around. The saloon was not quite as empty as the sheriff had said. Frank Keller was behind the bar, getting set up for the day, and he glowered at both of them.

"Lancaster, do you know a woman

named Margaret Adams?"

Lancaster frowned. His mind was fuzzy these days, usually filled with accusing blue eyes, especially when he'd been pulled from a deep sleep.

"I don't think so . . ."

"She got to town about a week ago. 'Sposed to be the new schoolteacher."

Lancaster shook his head.

"I don't know her."

"Pretty blond woman with a little girl."

Lancaster perked up at the mention of the child.

"She says you've been watchin' her, followin' her."

Lancaster didn't reply.

"Well, have you?"

Lancaster said something the sheriff didn't catch.

"What was that?"

"I said not her."

"Whataya mean, not her?"

"I've been watchin' the little girl."

"The little girl?" the sheriff repeated. "Whatsa matter, grown-up women don't appeal to you?"

Lancaster didn't answer.

"Come on, Lancaster, don't make this hard on yourself. Why you been watchin' a little girl?"

"I don't want anything to happen to her."

Sheriff Mathis thought about that and scratched his head.

"You got some reason to think that somethin' is gonna happen to her?"

"No," Lancaster said, "I just —"

"Never you mind 'I just,' " Sheriff Mathis said, "just stop it, all right? It don't look good havin' a grown man following a little girl around town."

"I just . . . want to keep her safe."

"That's my job, Lancaster," Mathis said, smacking his chest with his fist. "I get to keep the people in this town safe, not you."

"But —"

"No buts," Mathis said, cutting him off. "Look, if you don't stop I'm gonna have to run you out of town. The town council ain't gonna want you scarin' away their new schoolteacher. If it comes down to you or her, Lancaster, you're gone. You got that?"

Lancaster nodded.

"Yeah," he said, "I got it."

"Okay, then," Mathis said, "I'm done. Go back to sleep."

"He ain't goin' back ta sleep," Frank Keller said. "Now that he's up, he's gonna sweep this place out before we open . . . ain't ya, Lancaster?"

Lancaster waved a hand and stood up.

"Just let me get dressed," he said, and started back to his room.

"Remember what I said, Lancaster," the sheriff warned. "No more followin' women, or little girls . . . or anybody!"

Chapter Five

Josiah Alton was a hunter, pure and simple. When you wanted somebody found, you hired Alton, and that's what Aaron Delaware did. Alton was paid a lot of money to find Delaware's wife and daughter, and the hunter found them in Dunworthy, Texas.

Alton arrived in Dunworthy the day after the sheriff warned Lancaster away from Margaret Adams and her daughter, Alicia. He'd picked up Margaret "Adams'" trail in Missouri and followed it all the way down here to East Texas.

Alton took a room in the same hotel as Margaret and Alicia Adams and noticed the woman's name written in the register.

"Are there any kids stayin' in this hotel?" he asked the clerk.

"Well," the man said, "one, but she's very well behaved. I'm sure you won't have any trouble."

"That's okay," Alton said. "I like kids."

He signed in and went up to his room.

★ ★ ★

Alton watched Margaret and Alicia for the next two days, the same two days that Lancaster was trying *not* to watch them. If Lancaster had ignored the sheriff's warning, maybe things would have turned out different.

Before taking up watch on the woman and child, though, Alton went to the telegraph office and sent word back east to his employer: COME TO DUNWORTHY, TEXAS. BRING MY MONEY.

He signed it.

On the third day both men made a move that would affect everyone's future.

Lancaster couldn't take it anymore. He knew that if he tried to follow the woman and the child again the sheriff would run him out of town, but he had to do something. He decided to go to the hotel and talk to the woman, explain everything. He hoped she would understand.

At the same time, Josiah Alton decided to make his move. He left his hotel room, walked down the hall, and knocked on the door.

"Mrs. Delaware?" he said when she opened the door.

He could see by the look in her eyes that she was startled.

"I — I'm sorry," she stammered, "you must be mistaken. I'm not —"

"There's no mistake," Alton said, and pushed her inside.

"I — I'll scream," she threatened.

He smiled tightly.

"If you do," he said, "I'll hurt the child."

"Y-you wouldn't!"

"I would, Mrs. Delaware," he said. "Look at my face."

"Yes," Margaret Delaware said. His was the face of a killer, ugly and devoid of expression or even the *potential* for warmth. "I see you would. All right, what do you want?"

"Mommy —" Alicia said, in a tiny, frightened voice.

"Hush, honey. It's all right."

"Just to tell you that you've been found," Alton said, answering her question. "Your husband should be here by morning."

That soon, she thought. She had to get Alicia away from here at any cost.

"H-he hired you?"

"Yes."

"To do what?"

"To find both of you."

"Not to bring us back?"

"No," Alton said, "he wanted to come

44

and get you. Apparently, you've led him a merry chase, Mrs. Delaware. I'm the fourth man he hired to find you."

"And the best, no doubt."

He smiled, and by doing so made himself even uglier.

"No doubt."

Margaret turned her back to him and walked to the dresser.

"Please don't try anything, Mrs. Delaware."

She turned to face him.

"Isn't there anything I can say . . ."

"No."

". . . or do to change your mind?"

Alton looked her up and down. She was the most beautiful woman he'd ever seen. He'd been ugly all his life, and the only women he'd had were whores. There was something she could do, all right. It wouldn't change his mind, but it would make him happy.

"Sure," he said, "you're welcome to try. God, you're a beautiful woman!"

She took his meaning immediately, her eyes flicking to Alicia, who was sitting on the bed quietly, watching them both with wide eyes.

"Put her in the closet," Alton said.

"What?" Margaret jerked her eyes from Alicia to Alton.

"Put her in the closet," he said again. "She won't see nothing."

"But she'll hear —"

"Do it!" Alton said. "Or I will."

"All right," Margaret said, "all right."

She walked to her daughter and looked at her gravely.

"Come with me, honey."

The little girl got off the bed and took her mother's hand. Margaret led her to the closet door, and the girl balked.

"I don't want to go in the closet, Mommy."

"It'll be all right, honey."

"It'll be dark."

"Close your eyes, baby," she said. "Remember how Mommy told you if you close your eyes you can't see the dark?"

"I remember."

Margaret opened the door, and Alicia took small, halting steps until she was inside. The child sensed that something out of the ordinary was happening. Normal childhood fears did not apply here.

"Crouch down, baby," Margaret said, "and put your hands over your ears. Don't come out until Mommy opens the door, understand?"

"Yes, Mommy."

"I love you, honey," Margaret said, and closed the door.

She turned to face Josiah Alton, who had already unbuttoned his pants. He had done so without taking off his gunbelt.

"Get undressed!" he ordered. He was in a fever now, knowing that he was just moments away from having this woman, a woman who under normal circumstances wouldn't have even looked at him — would probably sooner spit on him than share a bed with him. Well, by God, he was going to show her. . . .

She walked back to stand in front of the dresser. On it was her purse. She started to undo her dress.

"What happens to you if I tell my husband what happened here today?" she asked.

Alton smiled that ugly smile again. The smugness of it made it even more offensive.

"He wouldn't believe you," Alton said. "You left him and took his daughter —"

"My daughter, too!" she said vehemently. He ignored her.

"To tell you the truth," he said, unbuttoning his shirt so she could see his monstrously hairy chest, "he doesn't even want you back. He wants the girl."

She turned away as she peeled her dress down to her waist.

"Don't be shy," he said.

"What will he do to me when he gets here?"

"If you ask me," Alton said, "he's mad enough to kill you."

"Then I guess I have nothing to lose," she said.

"Wha—"

She turned, holding a small two-shot derringer she had taken out of her purse when her back was to him.

"Damn," Alton said, and went for his gun.

Chapter Six

Lancaster was approaching the door to Margaret Adams's room when he heard the shots. One was faint, but the other was very clear. They both came from inside the room. Fearing for the safety of the child, he slammed his shoulder into the door, forcing it open.

The woman was down and the man in the room was staggering. Lancaster saw this in an instant and reacted. He threw himself at the man, who turned in time for Lancaster to hit him waist high with his shoulder. The two of them fell to the floor, the man's gun jarred from his hand by the impact.

Lancaster wasted no time. He went for the fallen gun and turned quickly.

Josiah Alton, hampered by the bullet from the derringer that had entered his shoulder, and jarred by the man who had burst into the room, rolled over and saw the man pointing the gun at him.

"Don't," Lancaster said, but Alton was beyond heeding the warning.

The fallen man lunged for Lancaster, who fired once. The bullet entered the man's chest, slamming him back down to the floor for good.

Lancaster rushed to the woman, who was now on her knees, blood dripping from a chest wound.

"Alicia—" she gasped. "My little girl—"

"Where is she?" Lancaster asked.

"C-closet," Margaret said.

"What happened here?"

"My . . . husband hired . . . man . . ."

"Your husband?"

"Bad man . . ." she said, her voice getting weaker, ". . . bad, bad . . . man."

Lancaster didn't know what to do for her except lower her into a prone position on the floor. She grabbed the front of his shirt in her bloody hand.

"Don't let him . . ."

"Don't let him what?"

"Don't . . . let him . . . get her . . ." the woman said painfully. "Please . . ."

"I won't," Lancaster promised. He took her hand, sticky with her blood, from his shirt, held it, squeezed it. "I won't."

"Prom—" she started, but she died before she could get the word out.

He knew what it was going to be, though.

50

"I promise," he said, lowering her hand to the floor.

He stared at her for a moment, then became aware of some noise outside. Apparently others had heard the commotion, too.

He stood up and strode across the room to the closet door, tucking the dead man's gun into his belt. He opened the door and the little girl was there, crouched down with her eyes tightly shut and her hands pressed to her ears. She sensed the light, though.

"Mommy?" she asked without opening her eyes. "Is it over?"

Chapter Seven

"The poor little thing," Cynthia Mathis said.

She and her husband were standing in the doorway of their spare room, looking at Alicia Adams, who was asleep. When Mathis had responded to the shooting in the hotel he'd done two things upon surveying the carnage in Margaret Adams's room. He arrested Lancaster and put him in jail, and he took the child home to his wife, who fell in love with her immediately. Mathis knew he was taking a chance exposing his wife to the little girl. They had tried for years to have a family, and had finally become resigned to the fact that they would not. This, he knew, might open old wounds for her.

"What will you do with her?" Cynthia asked.

"I don't know, dear," Mathis said. "That would be for the courts to decide, I suppose."

"Let's leave her be," Cynthia said, and they backed out of the room. She left the door open so they would be able to hear the child, and they went to the kitchen to have tea together.

When they were seated across from each other with tea and warm oatmeal cookies in front of them, she asked, "What about Lancaster?"

"He'll spend the night in jail," Mathis said. "I wasn't able to question the child today, but I will tomorrow."

They had summoned the doctor to the house to take a look at Alicia. He had pronounced her physically sound, but said she was in a state of shock.

"Don't try to ask her anything before tomorrow," he advised, and Mathis was adhering to that advice.

"Dan —"

"I know what you're going to say," he warned.

"Why did you bring her here, then?" she asked. "You knew very well I would fall in love with her the minute you walked in the door with her."

"Yes," he said, "I suppose I did, but I also knew you would take damned good care of her. That was what I was concerned with the most."

She reached out and took his hand, holding it tightly.

"Let's see what the courts say," he said to

her. "Maybe she has a father somewhere."

"All right," she said, "we'll wait and see."

She released his hand, and they went back to their tea and cookies.

In the morning Mathis went to the jail with breakfast for Lancaster and talked with him while he ate.

"So you don't deny killing the man?" Mathis asked.

"I had to," Lancaster said. "It was him or me. The woman was on the floor, wounded, and I didn't know where the little girl was."

"You sure there weren't any witnesses?"

"Not to what went on in the room, unless someone comes forward and says they saw everything."

"I'll talk to the hotel guests again," Mathis said, "but you know how people are. Nobody wants to be involved."

"Where is the little girl now?" Lancaster asked.

"She's all right," Mathis said. "She's at my house, with my wife."

"You can't let anything happen to her."

Mathis was surprised by Lancaster's vehemence.

"I don't intend to."

"I made a promise to her mother."

"Before she died?"

"Yes."

"To do what?"

"To keep her safe."

"Did she say anything about a father?"

Lancaster pushed away his breakfast tray and looked at Mathis.

"That's who she wanted me to keep her safe from!"

Mathis checked the register to see where the woman and child had come from. She had simply signed "Connecticut," and Mathis knew nothing of that eastern state. He knew, however, that without the name of a town there'd be no finding the little girl's father.

He spoke with the mayor, Alfred Collins, who had hired Margaret Adams to be the town schoolteacher. The mayor told him that the woman had contacted him by letter, stated her qualifications, and applied for the job. He had never spoken to her until she arrived in town.

When Mathis left the mayor's office it was to return home and finally question the little girl.

Cynthia and Dan Mathis were very surprised by the girl's calm and forthrightness.

She cleared Lancaster of any wrongdoing, saying that the man had come into their room, threatened her mother, and told her mother to put her in the closet. She had remained there until Lancaster opened the door. She spoke without any tremor in her voice, and had asked only once if her mother was "still dead."

She broke Cynthia Mathis's heart.

Sheriff Dan Mathis released Lancaster an hour later.

"How is she?" Lancaster asked before leaving the jail.

"The little girl? She's fine — maybe too fine. She hasn't cried."

"I'll be watching her."

"Lancaster —"

"If you hadn't warned me off, maybe this wouldn't have happened."

Mathis started to reply and then stopped, because the statement rang of truth.

"I have to keep her safe this time," Lancaster said, and left the sheriff's office.

Mathis wondered what "this time" meant.

Chapter Eight

A few days later the door to the sheriff's office opened and a man stepped in. He was the type of man Mathis had no use for. He dressed in a way that said "money" loud and clear, and he had that "money" look on his face, too.

Mathis had a bad feeling.

"Sheriff?"

"That's right," the lawman said. "Sheriff Dan Mathis."

"My name is Aaron Delaware."

"What can I do for you, Mr. Delaware?"

"I've just arrived in town, and I'm looking for some people."

"Who might they be?"

"One's a man named Josiah Alton," Delaware said, "and the other is my wife, Margaret."

"Margaret Adams?"

"Delaware," the man said, "Margaret Delaware — but she might be going by Adams. I'm also looking for my little girl, Alicia."

The bad feeling intensified.

"Mr. Delaware," Mathis said, "why don't you have a seat."

Aaron Delaware was upset.

The sheriff naturally assumed that the man was upset because his wife had been killed. Little did he know that Delaware cared nothing at all about that. To this successful eastern publishing mogul his wife was dead when she left him and took their daughter with her nine months before.

"Tell me again what happened."

"Well," Mathis said, "people who heard the shots and were in the hall saw Lancaster come out of your wife's hotel room, carrying a little girl."

"And then what happened?"

"Well . . . nothin'," the sheriff said again. "When I got there they were in the lobby. I went upstairs and found Alton and your wife dead. Your wife's dress — uh, apparently Alton was trying to . . ."

"Yes, yes," Delaware said, "I can guess what Alton was trying to do. Do you have this man Lancaster in custody?"

"I did," Mathis said, "but I let him go."

Delaware, a barrel-chested, florid-faced man in his forties, slammed a meaty fist down on the sheriff's desk. The sheriff was willing to let the act go without remark, because of the man's grief. Also, Mathis was intimidated by Delaware.

"Why?"

"He was cleared."

"By who?"

"By your daughter."

Delaware banged on the desk again.

"You questioned my daughter?"

"She was the only eyewitness."

"An eight-year-old girl?" Delaware asked. "You took her word?"

"Mr. Delaware," Mathis said, "near as I can figure, Lancaster probably saved your daughter's life."

"Where is my daughter now?"

"She's at my house," Mathis said, "with my wife."

"I want her."

"Uh, Mr. Delaware," Mathis said, "there are still some questions to be answered."

"What kind of questions?"

"About the, uh, other man? Alton?"

"What about him?"

"Well, was he working for you?"

"Yes."

"Looking for your wife?"

"Why would I have someone looking for my wife? I knew where she was. I was on my way here to meet with her."

"I see."

"Exactly how did all this happen again?"

"Near as I can figure," the sheriff said, "Lancaster must have come to the door just as Alton was killing your wife. The room looked like there was a scuffle, and Alton was shot twice. Once with your wife's derringer, and once with another gun — probably his own."

"You don't sound like you know very much for sure, Sheriff."

"That's why I'm still askin' questions, Mr. Delaware. You didn't answer me about Alton."

"I want my daughter, Sheriff," Delaware said, "and I don't want to have to answer a lot of questions in order to get her. Understood?"

Before Sheriff Mathis could offer an answer the man was gone, slamming the door behind him.

Aaron Delaware's anger was palpable. It cleared a path in front of him as he walked down the street. When he reached the hotel even the desk clerk, who was not in his path, shrank from him as he passed the desk on the way to the stairs.

In his room Delaware paced the floor.

He'd hired four men to find his wife and daughter since they'd disappeared, and Josiah Alton was the first to even find her trail. When he heard from Alton that he'd found Margaret and Alicia he had left Boston immediately for Texas, only to arrive and find both Alton and Margaret dead — and Alicia in the hands of the local law. He could not afford the sheriff's questions. He did not want it to get out that Alton was tracking his wife and daughter.

Even though he'd wanted a boy, and held Margaret responsible for not having one, he loved little Alicia. She was his blood, for God's sake. How could Margaret have taken her from him? She'd been free to go anytime she wanted to, she knew that, but she insisted that she wanted Alicia. Well, he'd told her in no uncertain terms the consequences she'd face if she fought him for custody.

He never suspected that she had the nerve to just leave and take Alicia with her. Oh, the dire consequences she would have faced when he found her — if she hadn't been killed first.

Sheriff Mathis sat back in his chair after Aaron Delaware stormed from his office and chided himself for letting the easterner intimidate him. It was not anything the man had said or done, but rather the man's money. Mathis had considered himself a poor man most of his life, and as such he was intimidated by men with money. They made him feel small, and he hated feeling small. Maybe that was why he had become a lawman. The badge made him feel bigger. Little had he known when he first picked up a badge that it would, more often than not, put him in contact with people with money. Usually, they were town merchants, minor politicians even, and over the years he had come to terms with those people.

Aaron Delaware, however, was a different story. Even here in Texas Mathis had heard about Delaware's publishing empire in the East. This man had the kind of money that would intimidate anyone, let alone a Texas sheriff.

Chapter Nine

Mayor Alfred Collins stared at Aaron Delaware, who was standing in front of his desk, and knew that this man might very well be his salvation, his way out of Dunworthy and into a political office that would take him to Washington, D.C. This was a dream of Collins's which — now that he was in his sixties — had been fading, but now, very suddenly, was vivid once again.

"Now," Delaware said, "I'm not trying to tell you how to run your town, Mayor —"

"Of course not."

"— but it seems to me your sheriff is going a little above and beyond his duties when he tries to keep my daughter from me."

"Yes, yes, I see," Collins said, although what he was seeing was in his head, and far off in the future. He was going to have to find himself a tailor and buy a whole new wardrobe.

"I'd simply like you to speak to the man for me," Delaware went on, "and show him the error of his ways."

"Of course, Mr. Delaware," Mayor Collins said, "that is certainly something I can do."

Delaware smiled.

"I knew you were a reasonable man, Mayor," he said, "and, of course, a leader by example."

"Yes, yes," Collins said, one eye on the present and one on the future, "I am, indeed. . . ."

"How do we know he's her father?" Mathis demanded of the mayor, who had marched into his office with his chest puffed out. Mathis knew that meant trouble. The mayor became self-important only when he was going to try to meddle in Mathis's job.

"He says he's her father," Collins said.

"And we're supposed to take his word for it?"

"What about the little girl, Sheriff?" Collins asked. "Will you take her word for it?"

"She's only eight years old."

"And yet you released Lancaster on her word," Collins pointed out.

Mathis frowned. The man had him there.

"All right, Mayor," Mathis said, "I'll put the little girl and Delaware together and we'll see what happens."

"If she says he's her father," Collins said,

"you're to turn her over to him. Is that understood?"

"Loud and clear, Mayor," Mathis said. He had suddenly realized what must be going on. A man like Alfred Collins would see a man like Aaron Delaware as a godsend. Delaware was Collins's way out of Dunworthy, and maybe even out of Texas.

"I think I understand you perfectly," he said, and the irony of the statement completely eluded the politician.

"Good," he said, "very good."

Mathis decided to go home and talk to his wife about what he had to do. He wasn't surprised when he arrived to see Lancaster standing across the street from his house, watching it.

"Lancaster," he said, crossing over to the man.

Lancaster, who had been leaning against the wall, straightened up and faced the sheriff.

"I didn't go near the house, Sheriff."

"I know," Mathis said, "it's fine. I'm not here to roust you."

Lancaster relaxed and leaned against the wall again.

"How is she?" he asked.

"She was fine this morning," Mathis said,

"but . . . her father's in town."

Lancaster straightened up again.

"Her father?"

Mathis nodded.

"His name's Aaron Delaware. He's the rich fella from the East, owns a publishing empire, lots of newspapers."

"What are you going to do?" Lancaster demanded.

"What can I do?" Mathis replied. "I have orders from the Mayor to put the two of them together. If the girl identifies him as her father . . ."

"You're going to give her to him?"

Mathis shrugged helplessly.

"I won't have much choice," he said. "Not if he's really her father."

"You can't do that!" Lancaster said. "She . . . she's afraid of him. He used to beat her mother, he sent that man after them . . . she won't want to go."

"She's a child, Lancaster," Mathis said. "A child belongs with her parents — in this case, her remaining parent."

"When are you going to do this?"

"I'll set it up for tomorrow afternoon," Mathis said. "I need time to talk to the little girl."

"You'll be putting her in danger," Lancaster said.

"He won't hurt her," Mathis argued. "He's her father, for Chrissake."

"Sheriff —"

"Lancaster," Mathis said, putting his hand on the man's arm, "I know what happened in Big Bend. Believe me, this is the best thing for you. You can't spend your whole life tryin' to protect one little girl because of what happened to another."

Lancaster did not reply.

"You better get over to the saloon before Frank Keller fires you."

Lancaster didn't move.

"Go on, now," Mathis said. "I'm tellin' you as a friend. Don't make me tell you as the sheriff."

Reluctantly, Lancaster turned and walked away.

Chapter Ten

Lancaster knew he was taking a chance, but there was no way he could allow the sheriff to give the little girl back to her father. Not after the promise he had made to her dying mother.

In watching the house as he had most of the day, he'd been able to discover what room she was in. After dark that night he sneaked up to the house and tapped lightly on her window. He hoped he wouldn't have to tap any harder. If he woke the sheriff he was going to be in real trouble.

Luckily, she was either a light sleeper or had been awake, because she came to the window and opened it. He was surprised to see that she was dressed.

"Hi, mister," she said. "I thought you forgot about me."

"No," Lancaster said, "I couldn't forget about you."

"I been waiting for you to come and take me away."

"Why is that?"

"The sheriff told me today he's gonna

give me back to my daddy."

"And you don't want that?"

She shook her head.

"He's a bad man," she said. "My mommy said we shouldn't be with him. She's still dead, isn't she?"

"Yes, honey," he said, touching her arm, "she's still dead."

"Then it's up to you," she said, "to keep me away from my daddy."

"You're all dressed," he said. "How did you know I'd come?"

She shrugged. "I just knew."

"Well," he said, reaching for her, "come on, then. Let's get you out of there and away from here before we wake the sheriff up. Do you have anything you want to take with you?"

"No."

"A doll," he said, "or some clothes?"

"No, nothing. I just want to go."

He lifted her out through the window and set her on the ground.

"Let's go, then."

She slipped her hand into his and looked up at him.

"Where?" she whispered.

"I haven't quite figured that out yet," he said honestly.

The first things he saw when he opened *his*

eyes the next morning were those blue eyes. They were staring down at him, wide and innocent, and filled with . . . what? Trust?

"Mister?" Alicia said.

"Wha—"

"Mister, you gotta wake up." She put a hand tentatively on his shoulder, then got brave and shook him.

"Huh?"

"It's time to get up."

"Ohhh . . ." Lancaster moaned as he rolled over. It had been a while since he'd slept on the ground — not that the pallet he had been sleeping on lately was much better.

"I'm hungry," she said.

He propped himself up on an elbow and looked at her.

"You are, huh?"

She nodded emphatically.

"Well, then," he said, "let's see what we can do about it."

Painfully, he got to his feet and went to the fire. It had gone out during the night, so he started it up again. While he made a pot of coffee for himself, and some bacon for her, he reflected on the occurrences of the day before.

He was still kind of groggy, but he remembered that from the moment he'd lifted the little girl out of the window they'd been on the go. They had gone straight to his room behind the saloon, entering from the back. He'd collected his own belongings from the trunk where he kept them, pausing only when he lifted out his gunbelt. He stared at it, hefted it, then finally strapped it on.

"What's wrong?" she asked.

He smiled at her and said, "It's just been a while since I wore this."

"Why?"

"I haven't needed it."

"And now you do?" she asked. "To protect me?"

"We're going to be on the road, little one," he said. "I'll need it to protect both of us."

"My name's Alicia."

"I know," he said, "Alicia. I'll use it from now on. Okay?"

"Okay."

Before going to the sheriff's house he had picked up some supplies. He'd made his decision to snatch the girl — Alicia — right after talking to the sheriff about her father. He'd spent the rest of the day getting ready.

He picked up a canvas bag that he'd packed with their necessaries and took the little girl out back again, where his horse was saddled and tied.

"Don't I get a horse?" she asked.

"You'll have to ride with me, Alicia," he said. "Grabbing you was bad enough, I don't want anyone coming after me for being a horse thief."

He lifted her up into the saddle, then climbed up behind her. He settled them both in comfortably, then tied the sack to the saddle horn.

"Do we still not know where we're going?" she asked.

"Nope," he said. "All we know is that we're going."

Now he struggled to clear his head and remember how far they had come before they stopped. Alicia had fallen asleep on the horse, seated in front of him, and had not awakened when he lowered her to the ground and covered her with a blanket. He'd built a fire, had some coffee, and fallen asleep next to her.

He looked around them, but the place where they were camped really didn't look familiar. As near as he could figure they must have ridden for four or five hours in the dark. They had to be about ten or fifteen miles north of Dunworthy.

When the bacon was done he put it in a plate and handed it to her.

"Be careful, it's hot."

"Aren't you gonna eat?"

"I'm just having coffee."

"What's your name?" she asked him. It had not come up until now.

"Lancaster."

"That's all? Just Lancaster?"

"That's all."

"Your mommy didn't give you another name?"

"I don't use it."

"What is it?"

"Never mind that," he said. "Tell me about your mother and father."

She put her head down.

"They don't get along — I mean, they *didn't* get along very well."

"Why not?"

"My mother . . . she told me that my father was a cruel man."

They had touched on that before, but Lancaster wanted to know more.

"She told you that?"

She nodded gravely. "She even said he was evil."

"Did you believe her?"

"Yes," she said. She looked up at him now with those blue eyes. "My mother never lied to me, mister."

"And did your father lie?"

"All the time," she said. "To me, to Mommy, and to other people. Mommy finally said we couldn't live there anymore."

"Why not?"

She looked down at her plate.

"My father used to hit her."

Lancaster had no respect for a man who beat a woman, no matter what else he had done, good or bad.

"Alicia, the man who . . . shot your mother. Why do you say he was sent by your father?"

"He told her," Alicia said. "I heard it when I was in the closet. I . . . I was supposed to not be listening, but I did. Is that all right?"

"That's fine, Alicia," he said soothingly. "You did just fine."

Lancaster thought about asking her why she was in the closet, but he remembered that her mother's dress had been down around her waist. He could guess the rest.

"Do you have any other family?"

"No," the child said sadly. Then she brightened and looked up at him. "Do you?"

The question caught Lancaster off guard.

"Uh, well, no, I don't —"

74

"Then you could be my new family," she said. "You could be my new daddy."

"I don't know, Alicia," he said. "I mean, you need a mother . . ."

"You could marry somebody," she said, proud that she had come up with the answer, "and she could be my new mommy."

"Alicia," he said, "you can't replace a mother or a father that easily."

Or, he thought, a child. He was thinking about the woman whose child he had killed, the little girl with blue eyes.

"Besides," he added, "you already have a father."

"I don't like him anymore," she said stubbornly. "He hurt my mommy, and he sent that man to kill her. You saved my life. I want *you* for my daddy."

Lancaster stared down at the little girl and realized that to her, her logic was infallible. Hell, it even sounded right to him, but . . . he couldn't be anyone's father. He wasn't even a whole man, he was all broken inside . . . unless . . .

"How old are you, Alicia?"

"I'm eight years old."

How old was that girl in Big Bend? he wondered. She had to have been around eight. He wondered what her mother was doing now.

Alicia finished her food and set the plate aside carefully.

"Where will we go?"

"I'm still not sure, Alicia, but we'll have to get going soon."

"Are they going to come after us?"

"Oh, yes," Lancaster said, "they are definitely going to come after us."

Chapter Eleven

They left soon after Alicia finished her break-fast. Lancaster knew they were going to have to stop someplace else to stock up on supplies. Of course, he wouldn't know what and how much to buy until he knew where they were headed.

Not ever having been a father, Lancaster had no concept of what it entailed, what it felt like. He also had no idea about whether or not a father could harm his own child.

Apparently, Alicia's father was able to harm his wife, but what about the little girl? She had the same blood he had. Did that make a difference?

If Alicia's father could have his own wife killed, could Lancaster — in all good conscience — ever give the girl back to him?

Who was he to judge? Hadn't he killed a little girl in Big Bend? Accident or not, he'd taken the life of a child just like Alicia.

He thought again about the girl in Big Bend, and the mother. He never did see the mother after the incident. He remembered her only from passing her in the street. He didn't even know if he would recognize her if he ever did see her again. What he did remember, however, was the anguished scream when she realized her daughter was dead.

He often heard that scream in his dreams.

What if, he thought, he took Alicia to that mother? He knew he could never replace her own child, but wouldn't it do Alicia some good? It certainly seemed a better option to him than giving her back to her father. Who knew what he would do to her?

Funny, he thought as he stared down at the top of the little girl's head, he never thought he'd ever go back to Big Bend, Kansas. He'd never even *thought* about going back there, but now . . . it really seemed the only course of action. It would help Alicia, it might help the grieving mother . . . and maybe it would help him. Maybe it would take away the nightmares, maybe it would enable him to get on with living his life instead of just hanging on.

He knew his reception in Big Bend would not be a good one. Certainly not from the sheriff, or from the mother. But this child needed help, and for the life of him, Lancaster could not think of anything else to do with her.

He certainly couldn't keep her himself.

From now on, though, he knew he'd have to keep watch, because they would doubtless be coming after him. Hopefully, he could get Alicia to Big Bend, Kansas, before anyone — the law or her father — caught up with them.

Once the child was safe, he didn't care if they found him or not.

Chapter Twelve

When the sheriff looked up from his desk and saw Aaron Delaware enter his office with Mayor Collins, he knew he was in trouble.

"Sheriff."

"Mayor."

Delaware remained silent, but he had a smug look on his face. Mathis had seen the look before. It was the look of a man who has a politician in his pocket, even if it was a minor one.

"Well," Mayor Alfred Collins said, "Mr. Delaware is ready to see his daughter?"

"Uh," Mathis said, "there's a, uh, problem with that, Mayor."

"What kind of problem?" Delaware asked. "What are you trying to pull, Sheriff?"

"What's going on, Dan?" the mayor asked. "This man has a right to see his daughter."

"I agree, Mayor."

"Then what's the problem?"

"I, uh, don't have her anymore."

"What?"

"Where is she?" Collins asked.

"I don't know."

"This is outrageous!" Delaware shouted. "What the hell do you mean you don't know where she is?"

"When we woke up this morning she was gone," Mathis said. "Apparently, she went out a window."

"By herself?" the mayor asked.

"No," Mathis said, "it looks like somebody helped her. There were some tracks outside the window."

"Tracks?" Collins asked.

"A man's boot prints."

"That madman!" Delaware shouted. "What's his name? Lancaster? He took her."

"Was it Lancaster?" Collins asked.

"Well . . . he's not around, either, and his horse is gone —"

"I knew it! I'll have your job, you incompetent — I want his badge, Mayor!"

Collins was distressed. He could not afford to have Aaron Delaware this angry, and yet he had no one to replace Mathis with if he took his badge.

"Mr. Delaware," he said calmly, "can we step outside for a moment?"

"What the hell —"

"I really think it would be better if we stepped outside."

Grudgingly, Delaware agreed. Mathis remained inside, wondering what kind of deal the mayor was making.

Collins was the man who had hired him eight years earlier, and since then Mathis had won six terms of reelection — as had Collins. The sheriff knew, however, that Alfred Collins, at sixty-five, still had ambitions of bigger and better things in politics. He also knew that a man like Aaron Delaware, who had money and power, could offer Collins the help he needed.

After a few moments the door opened and both Delaware and the mayor stepped back in.

"Sheriff," Mayor Collins said, "I've assured Mr. Delaware that you will be forming a posse to go after the man who stole his daughter."

"That's not for me to do, Mayor," Mathis said. "You need Federal help on this."

"Nevertheless," Collins said, "I want you to do it, before Lancaster gets further away."

Mathis frowned at Collins and asked, "Can we talk without him in the room?"

Delaware answered before the mayor could.

"I'll be happy to wait outside, Alfred." Delaware looked very satisfied with himself.

Mathis waited until Delaware had left the office before speaking.

"Alfred?" he said. "You're on a first-name basis already?"

"He can do a lot for this town, Dan," Mayor Collins argued.

"You mean a lot for you, don't you, Mayor?" Mathis asked. "What's he gonna do, make you a congressman? A senator?"

"Dan," Mayor Collins said, "he can do you some good, too."

"All I want to do is my job, Alfred," Mathis said. "That's all I've ever wanted to do."

"Then do it," Collins said. "What about that little girl?"

"What about her?"

"What do you think Lancaster will do to her?"

"He won't hurt her, Alfred," Mathis said. "He's not that kind of man."

"How do you know what kind of man he is? He's only been here six months."

"I checked him out," Mathis said. "He used to live by his gun, but something happened in Big Bend, Kansas, that changed all that."

"What happened?"

Suddenly, Mathis knew he'd said too much.

"He killed a little girl."

"By God, Dan —"

"It was an accident, the way I hear it," Mathis said quickly. "She crossed between him and another man."

"I don't care how it happened," Collins said.

"Alfred, that little girl didn't want to see her father," Mathis said. "You should have seen her face last night when I mentioned him. She's afraid of him, and I think Alton worked for him."

"Sheriff, I want —"

"Alfred," Mathis said, "I think it's entirely possible this man had his own wife killed. Do you understand?"

"You get a posse together, Dan," Collins said firmly, "or I'll get someone who will."

"Are you threatening my job, Mayor?"

"That's what I'm doing, Dan," Collins said. "I'll have your badge, and you know I can do it."

Dan Mathis was very partial to his badge, and his job. This town was his home.

He sighed.

"All right, Mayor," he said reluctantly, "tell your benefactor he'll get his posse."

"Good."

Collins started for the door, then turned and said, "One more thing."

"What's that?"

"He'll be going along."

Mathis stared at the door as it closed behind the mayor, then shook his head and said in disgust, "Great."

The next day Sheriff Mathis collected his posse, which included three men from town, Aaron Delaware, and two men he had hired the day before. He had one deputy, and he was leaving him behind, in charge.

While Dunworthy was not a big town, it was a growing town, and growing towns attracted people of all occupations, like the gambler who had gotten off the stage with Margaret "Adams" Delaware.

Two such men were Fred Brown and Tom Sullivan. Both men were experienced bounty trackers, and had come to Dunworthy to see if there was any work. They had met Aaron Delaware the day before in the saloon, drawn there because they heard that someone was looking for a couple of good men.

When they entered the saloon and stopped at the bar, Aaron Delaware had been pointed out to them. He was seated at a back table, interviewing men. In fact, at that moment there was a man seated across from him.

Brown and Sullivan walked over to the

85

table, took hold of the man by his arms, heaved him out of the chair and tossed him almost halfway across the room. Then they looked down at Aaron Delaware, who was staring at them in surprise.

"We hear you're lookin' for a couple of men," Brown said.

"That's correct."

"To do what?" Sullivan asked.

Delaware studied the two of them for a moment and decided to be honest.

"To do what I want them to do."

"How much are you payin'?" Brown asked.

Delaware told them. It was more than either man had ever seen before.

"What can you do?" Delaware asked.

"For that kind of money?" Brown replied. "Just about anything."

"Just *about* anything?"

Brown shrugged, and Sullivan said, "It's negotiable."

"You're hired," Delaware said.

"I thought a posse was made up of townspeople," Eric Gates said. He *was* one of the townspeople.

"Not this time, Eric," Mathis said. "Mr. Delaware, there, is a special friend of the mayor's. It was his little girl that Lancaster took. That entitles him to come along, and to bring some help."

"It does?"

"That's what the mayor says."

Gates shook his head.

"I don't know Lancaster that well, Sheriff," he said, "but he don't strike me as the kind of man to steal a little girl."

"No," Mathis said, "me neither."

"What do we do when we find him?" Gates asked.

"Bring him back, I guess," Mathis said. "Him and the girl."

Gates looked over at Aaron Delaware and the two men with him. The two men wore their guns like they knew how to use them. They were in their thirties, their eyes hard and their faces stern. The sheriff had never heard of them, but he knew professionals when he saw them.

"Those two don't look like they're plannin' on bringin' him back."

"I noticed that, myself," Mathis said, wishing he had more men along. The way it stood now, he had three and Delaware had two, and while his three were fine for a posse, Delaware's two looked like they had done more gunwork.

It didn't seem all that even.

Chapter Thirteen

Over the course of the next three days Lancaster found his progress impeded by two things. One, the little girl was not used to traveling by horseback, and they had to rest periodically for her. The second thing was more personal. It had been months since Lancaster himself had been on the trail, and he was not in good enough physical shape to make the trip easily. He found that they had to stop for him to rest almost as often as for her.

He had thought that she could sleep in the saddle, but she only napped fitfully. When she was awake she asked questions.

"Where are we going?"

"When will we get there?"

"Are we there yet?"

"Will my daddy catch us?"

The last one was a hard one to answer. Lancaster was sure that a wealthy, influential man like her father — whose name she said was Aaron Delaware — would not take kindly to having his daughter taken away.

He also knew by doing so he was probably committing some terrible crime. Still, if the little girl was to be believed about her father, he felt he had no choice. Also, he had come to think of Alicia's safety as his redemption of sorts. He couldn't bring back the little girl he had killed, but he could make sure that nothing happened to this one.

So Delaware and whoever he was able to recruit would be on their trail, and were probably moving faster than they were owing to their frequent rest periods. Lancaster damned the shape his body was in. At night he found his hands shaking, and when he tried to hold them between his knees to stop them he found *them* shaking, as well. The long months of abuse he had heaped on his body was coming back to haunt him.

To the question of whether or not her father would catch up to them he replied, "I don't know, honey. I guess he'll try."

"But will he?"

He stared across the campfire at her.

"We'll just have to wait and see."

"But, Lancaster —"

"It's time for you to go to sleep now, Alicia."

"And you?"

"I'll be going to sleep, too."

She rolled over and wrapped herself in her

blanket. He was amazed at how much she had come to trust him — and he felt that he was betraying her trust because he could not remain on watch. It was impossible to stay awake all night and ride all day. He had to take the chance of getting some sleep, or risk falling asleep in the saddle and falling off his damn horse. He could break his neck that way, or hers.

Tonight he was pleased to find that his hands were not shaking as much as they had been the last few nights. Maybe the meager meals they were sharing were doing him some good. Also, he had drunk no alcohol since leaving town with her. He was surprised that his body was not craving it more, but maybe he hadn't been as far gone on whiskey as he had thought.

It was a chilly night, and he knew if he felt it, so did she. He took his blanket and put it on her while she slept, so that the chill would not wake her up. Then he sat closer to the fire to keep himself as warm as he could.

He sat with his gun in his hand, and soon his head drooped and his eyes closed.

"We're gettin' closer," Fred Brown said. He had one knee on the ground and was studying the tracks left behind by Lancaster.

"He's not doin' anythin' to hide his tracks," Sullivan said.

"I noticed," Brown replied.

"What's that mean?" Delaware asked.

Brown looked up at his employer.

"It means he probably expects us to catch up to him, sooner or later."

"Then why keep going?" Delaware asked.

"From what the sheriff tells me," Brown said, "the man is givin' himself no choice. He's going to keep goin' as long as he can."

"What about my daughter?" Delaware asked. "Is there any sign of her?"

"Some," Brown said. "She's with him."

"Good."

Mathis studied Aaron Delaware. The man might have loved his little girl, but the sheriff thought there was more pride than love behind his desperation to find her. He didn't believe for a minute that the woman had come here to meet him. More likely she had come here to get away from him, and he was upset that she had taken their daughter with her. Delaware was the kind of man who prized possessions above all else, and to him the little girl was a possession.

Sheriff Mathis wished he could prove that the man who killed Margaret Delaware — the woman he had known as Margaret Adams — had been working for Aaron Delaware. He suspected it — hell, he *knew* it — but he couldn't prove it. If he could, he would have thrown the man's ass in jail. What kind of man has his own wife killed?

"How far behind them are we?" Delaware asked.

Brown mounted up.

"A day, maybe a little more."

"Then this time tomorrow we might be right behind him."

"It's possible," Tom Sullivan said. "He's heading due north, towards Oklahoma or Kansas. It's my guess that's where he's headed."

"Why do you say that?" Delaware asked.

"Because if he's not bothering to cover his trail he thinks he's going to get to his destination before we catch up to him. That means it ain't gonna be that far. Oklahoma seems like a good bet, Kansas after that."

"You could be wrong," Mathis said.

Delaware looked at the lawman.

"And why do you say that?" he asked, almost with disdain.

Sullivan and Brown only stared at Mathis without saying a word.

"Because I know Lancaster," Mathis said. "He's too smart to be leaving this clear a trail."

"Maybe you give him too much credit,"

Delaware said. "From what I hear he was almost your town drunk."

"Ask your men about him," Mathis suggested.

Delaware looked at Brown and Sullivan in turn.

"Do you know this man?"

"We've heard of him," Brown said, answering for both of them. "Up until about six months ago he had a pretty good reputation."

"As what?" Delaware asked.

"As the kind of man you might hire to get something done, Mr. Delaware," Brown said.

"And now?"

Brown shrugged.

"We hadn't heard too much about him until you hired us," he said.

"I don't think he has a very good reputation now," Delaware said. "Not from what I heard around town." He looked at the sheriff. "Let's not make this more difficult than it should be, Sheriff."

"I won't . . ." Mathis said.

"Good."

". . . but Lancaster might."

Chapter Fourteen

"What's wrong?" Alicia asked. She was craning her neck to look up at Lancaster, who had turned in the saddle to look behind them.

"Some things you don't lose, I guess," he said.

"Like what?"

He looked down at her and said, "You're going to hurt your neck." At that moment he didn't want to be looking down into her eyes.

"What did you lose?" she asked, facing front again.

"It's what I didn't lose, kid," he said. "I get the feeling we're being followed."

"You said they would come after us, didn't you?"

"Yeah, I did," Lancaster said, "but this is a feeling like somebody's breathing down my neck."

"You mean like a ghost?"

The word "ghost" startled him for a moment.

"No," he said, "not a ghost, a real person. Somebody's tracking us."

"Are they going to catch us?"

He patted her head and said, "Not if I can help it."

"Can I hold the reins?"

"Have you ever been on a horse before, Alicia?"

She shook her head and said, "Only with you."

He let her hold the reins for a while, although he held her arms. He also gave her some instruction on how to ride, all the while thinking that he had to do something to throw the trackers off the trail. He had the feeling — given what the little girl said about her father, as well as what the sheriff had said — that there was a group chasing them that was part posse and part paid bounty hunters. Up to now he had taken no steps to hide their trail, but that was going to have to change, even before they reached Oklahoma. If he could lose them here in Texas he wouldn't have to worry about them in Oklahoma, and then Kansas.

Around dinnertime the solution came to him. All he had to do was find what he was looking for.

"I'm hungry," Alicia said a couple of

hours later. "Are we going to stop to eat?"

"Soon," he said. He took out a piece of beef jerky and gave it to her. "Here, chew on this for a while."

She gave him back the reins and held the jerky in two hands. She bit a piece off with difficulty and started chewing it.

"Why haven't we stopped yet?" she asked.

"I'm looking for something."

"What?"

At that moment he spotted it off in the distance.

"That."

She stared ahead and said, "I don't see anything."

"Look higher, in the sky."

She did, and said, "I see smoke."

"That's what I've been looking for."

"Why?"

"Because where there's smoke there's people," he said, "and where there's people there's horses."

"Huh?" she asked, still chewing.

"Never mind," he said. "Just listen up. Are you a good actress?"

"Actress?"

"When you wanted something from your mom that she didn't want you to have, did you put on an act?"

"Well . . ." she said.

"Come on, fess up."

"Sometimes I'd act, you know, real sad?"

"And pout?"

"Sometimes," she murmured, then said more loudly, "but mostly when I wanted a licorice or something."

"Well, if there's a camp with lots of people up ahead," he said, "here's what I want you to do. . . ."

He explained his plan to her — at least, her end of it — and then asked, "Can you do that?"

She craned her neck to look up at him again, but this time he only had to look at one eye, because she had the other one closed against the sun.

"Isn't that dishonest?" she asked.

"A little," he said, "but think of it like wanting to get a licorice."

She faced front, thought a moment, then said, "I think I can do that."

"Great," he said. "We're getting closer to the smoke. I just hope this is really what I'm looking for."

Whoever was tracking them had to be moving faster than they had been. It wouldn't be long before they caught up. This was the only way he could think of to throw them off the trail — if it worked.

★ ★ ★

As they got closer to the source of the smoke Lancaster saw that their luck was even better than he had thought. It was a large camp, and there were several fires. There was much commotion, with tents, buckboards, a string of horses, and — to his great satisfaction — there were women and children, as well.

He only hoped that he didn't look too disheveled and disreputable to pull off his plan — although most of it depended on Alicia.

Chapter Fifteen

As Lancaster rode into camp he studied the faces of the people who were watching him. He was looking for the right person, preferably a woman. If this had been a more conventional overnight camp with just a few men in it, he might not have even ridden in. You have to be careful when you ride up on a group of strangers, but this camp seemed to have families in it. It was a safe bet they'd react the way he wanted them to, especially to Alicia.

He finally picked out a woman, middle-aged with a kind, round face, and reined his horse in front of her.

"Ma'am."

The woman took one look at Alicia and said, "You poor dear, you look exhausted."

"Yes'm," Alicia said, her voice barely audible.

She was a natural, Lancaster thought, wishing he could see the look she had on her face at that moment.

"Ma'am," Lancaster said, "we'd take it as

a favor if you'd let us rest a spell."

"Well, landsakes, of course you can rest here, mister," the woman said. "This child looks half starved — and so do you, come to think of it."

"I had some beef jerky," Alicia said loudly. She made it sound as if it was the best thing she ever ate.

"Beef jerky?" the woman asked, frowning. "Child, what you need is some beef stew!"

"Rebecca?"

It was a man's voice, and the owner came over and stood next to the woman.

"Who is this man?" he asked.

"Husband, this is a stranger, and he and his little girl need to rest and have some hot food. I told him we wouldn't turn him away."

Lancaster noticed that the man was not wearing a gun.

"Where you be from, stranger?" the man asked.

"Well, sir, we've been riding a spell from South Texas and we haven't had much in the way of hot food."

"We don't have much money," Alicia chimed in.

The child was brilliant, he thought. Her timing was perfect.

"Sir, if you please," the man said, "I

would appreciate it if you would hand me your gun before you step down."

"Husband —"

"Hush, Rebecca," the man said. "We're in a savage land, and we don't know who this man is."

Lancaster looked around but could not see any armed men, so he felt there was no immediate danger. The only threat would come if the posse happened to catch up to them while they were in this camp and he was unarmed.

"I don't see any guns in camp," he commented.

"We keep them hidden away," the man said, "unless we need them to hunt with."

"What about protection?"

"The Lord provides that," the man said, and it all became clear to Lancaster. They were religious people, and that would work even more in his favor. He didn't much believe in religion, and probably wouldn't have known one from another, so he didn't think to ask them about theirs.

"Sir?" the man said. "Would you hand down your gun, please? We will return it when you leave. We do not like to have armed men around our children."

"Well, sir," Lancaster said, drawing the gun from his holster, "of course I'll do that, then, since you're being so hospitable."

The man, a tall fellow with long hair and a beard but — curiously — no mustache, stepped forward and accepted Lancaster's Colt.

"Now hand that child down to me, sir," the woman said, reaching for Alicia, "and we'll get the both of you fed."

"I'm much obliged, ma'am," Lancaster said, "much obliged for your kindness."

He handed Alicia down to the woman and then dismounted, mindful of the man's attention on him. He seemed to be the center of attention for most of the other people in camp, as well, at least the ones who weren't seeing to chores at the moment.

He noticed that the people were dressed alike, simple clothes, no weapons, no adornments of any kind. He and Alicia had really lucked into it when they found this camp. Now he only had to hope that the last part of his plan went as well.

As it turned out Lancaster had chosen well when he reined in his horse in front of Rebecca Sloan. Her husband, Silas, was the leader of these people, whose religion he still did not know. It didn't really matter, however. All that mattered was that he and Alicia were eating some of the best beef stew he'd ever had.

"This is excellent, Mrs. Sloan," he said.

"It's really good, ma'am," Alicia agreed. She was gulping it down like she hadn't eaten in months, and Lancaster wasn't so sure that it was an act.

Lancaster thought to ask if they had any whiskey, but he decided not to. They probably would not, and he really didn't need it anyway. He'd gone more days without whiskey than he had in months, and he didn't want to spoil that, even though his mouth and throat and belly craved it.

So he made do with coffee, which was also excellent.

Silas and Rebecca sat with them while they ate, and Silas questioned them. Others who were curious about the strangers came over, but Sloan shooed them away. As the leader it seemed as if he didn't want the others to come in contact with the strangers until he had checked them out. He seemed to be trying to trip Lancaster up somehow, and Lancaster wondered if all religious people were this curious.

Or was it suspicion?

"Is this your daughter?" Silas asked.

"Yes, sir," Lancaster said, "and the apple of my eye she is, too."

As if on cue Alicia leaned over and

pressed herself against Lancaster's knee, smiling at the Sloans. Lancaster thought this child must have gotten fistfuls of licorice when she wanted it.

"And where's your mother, little one?" Rebecca asked.

"Where'd you say she was, Pa?" Alicia asked Lancaster.

"Kansas, sweetie," he said to Alicia, then turned his attention to the Sloans. "Her mother's in Kansas, and we're on the way to meet her."

"Why isn't she traveling with you?" Rebecca asked.

"Oh, she went on ahead, ma'am, to take up her new position as schoolteacher. I put her on a stage, you see."

"And why didn't Alicia go with her?" Rebecca asked.

"That would seem to have been a better idea than having her ride with you," Silas Sloan said. "This seems hard on the child."

"Well, sir, I didn't have money for all of us to go by stage," Lancaster said. "And we did have a buggy we were traveling in, but we were set upon by bandits, who took it from us. We had to walk to the next town, where I used the remainder of our money — I had some hidden in my boot, you see — to buy this horse and rig."

"What a shame!" Rebecca said, clapping her hands together. "Child, you must have been frightened out of your wits."

"Yes'm," Alicia said. "I thought they were going to kill us. May I have some more stew?"

"Well, of course you can. You can have all you want. Come with me and we'll get it."

Alicia looked at Lancaster as if he was really her father and she needed his approval.

"Go on, honey," Lancaster said with as big a smile as he could give her. "These people are our friends."

The little girl got up with feigned reluctance and allowed the woman to shoo her along.

"She is an adorable child," Silas Sloan said.

"Yes, she is. Favors her mother."

"Yes," Sloan said, "I noticed there was very little resemblance between you."

"I count that as a blessing for a girl," Lancaster said, "don't you, Mr. Sloan?"

Sloan studied Lancaster for a few moments and then said, "Please, call me Silas."

That's when Lancaster knew his plan would work perfectly.

Chapter Sixteen

After they had eaten, Lancaster forced himself to wait a couple of hours before putting the remainder of his plan into effect. During that time Alicia spent a lot of time with Rebecca Sloan, who took her around and introduced her to the other children, including three of her own.

In turn some of the other adults were now allowed to approach Lancaster and talk to him. They were as curious as children, for the most part, but it was still Silas Sloan who came up with the most telling questions.

"If you don't mind me asking . . . ," he began.

"Please, Silas," Lancaster said, "after accepting your hospitality you can ask me anything."

"Well, you seem to me to be a man who . . . who knows how to use his gun. I do not mean to be insulting, here."

"No, it's all right," Lancaster said. "You're right, for a long time I was a man who used his gun quite often, but that was a while ago. I've been . . . ill, deathly ill, and being that close to death changes a man."

"Yes, you do seem to be . . . somewhat thin."

"But I'm putting the weight back," Lancaster said, touching his flat stomach — flat, but slightly swollen with Rebecca Sloan's stew. "Your wife's cooking has started fattening me up already, I think."

"My Rebecca," Sloan said proudly, "she is a wonderful cook."

"You still had a question you wanted to ask me?"

"Yes, I was wondering how these, uh, thieves were able to take your wagon, and your horse, and your money, and you did not ever use your gun."

Lancaster sensed that his answer to this question might finally gain him Sloan's trust.

"Silas, I was this close to risking it," he said, "but there were three of them, and I just felt that I had a better chance of getting Alicia out of that situation alive and unhurt by giving them what they wanted, and not resisting. I guess I just felt that violence was not the way."

"Brother Lancaster," Sloan said after a moment, "that is the rule we live by."

"Well, then," Lancaster said, "I guess I'm closer to being one of you than I ever thought I could be, sinner that I've been in the past."

"The past is past," Sloan said. "Praise the Lord, he forgives us."

"Amen," Lancaster said, hoping he hadn't pushed this thing *too* far.

"But why must you leave?" Rebecca asked Lancaster again.

"This little one is in a hurry to see her mother," Lancaster said to Rebecca.

"Surely you could stay the night?"

"I wouldn't want to impose on you any further, Rebecca," Lancaster said. "You good folks have been too kind to us already."

"Nonsense," she said, "there's no such thing as being too kind — and I love having Alicia around."

Just for a moment it occurred to Lancaster how well off Alicia would be with these people. He could leave her with them and continue on, drawing their pursuers farther and farther away from her. In the end, though, he decided against it. There was a woman in Big Bend who could use Alicia just as much as Alicia could use her.

"No, ma'am," Lancaster said, "we'll just get on our old horse and hope he sees us through to the end of our journey."

"What's wrong with your horse?" she asked, showing concern.

"Well, ma'am, he's just mighty tired, and he has been carrying two — not that Alicia weighs all that much, but when a horse is tired every pound counts."

Rebecca leaned forward, patted Lancaster's arm, and said, "You just wait right here."

She got up and went off, leaving him seated in front of the tent she shared with her husband. Alicia came walking over and sat by him.

"Did I do good, Lancaster?"

"Sweetie," he said, "you did great."

"Where's the lady going?"

"If I'm not mistaken," he said, "I believe she's going to get us a fresh horse."

"And that was the plan, wasn't it?" she asked.

"Yep," he said, "that was the plan."

"Lancaster?"

"Yes?"

"Do you feel bad about fooling these people?"

He looked down at her and winced at how piercing her eyes were.

"Yes, Alicia," he said honestly, "I do feel bad about it, but it was necessary. We needed another horse, so we wouldn't be leaving the same tracks behind us."

"Will they get in trouble for having your horse, now?"

"No," Lancaster said. "They're traveling west, according to the Sloans, into New Mexico and then Arizona. It won't take the people who are after us long to decide that they're going the wrong way, and then they'll turn back."

"Will they find our trail?"

"Maybe," Lancaster said, "and maybe not. Even if they do, though, it won't matter, because we'll have enough of a head start on them to get where we're going."

"Do you know where we're going now, Lancaster?" Alicia asked.

He hadn't told her the decision he'd come to days before.

"Yes, I think I do, Alicia."

"And will they help us there, too?"

"Yes," he said, "they will."

"And we won't have to pretend?"

"No, we won't."

"Good," she said. "Pretending is sometimes fun, but not this time."

"I know what you mean, Alicia."

Silas Sloan came walking over with his

110

wife, leading a fresh horse with Lancaster's saddle on it.

"We want you to take this animal," Sloan said. "We will accept yours in return."

Lancaster looked the horse over. It had some miles on it, but it was sound. He examined it and found that it was a gelding, probably eight or nine years old. Lancaster's dun was six, and rangier than this well-muscled gelding.

"Silas, I don't know what to say. . . ."

"Just take it," Sloan said, handing Lancaster the reins.

"It's a fine animal," Lancaster said.

"And I've packed some food for you," Rebecca said. "It's in your canvas sack."

"Thank you, Rebecca."

Rebecca crouched down and said to Alicia, "I wish we had more time to spend together, Alicia. You're a very sweet little girl."

Embarrassed, because she had been putting on an act for these people, Alicia looked away, and Rebecca took it for shyness. She grabbed the child and hugged her tightly.

Lancaster shook hands with Sloan, who then gave him his gun back. Lancaster mounted the gelding, which was several hands taller than his dun, then accepted

Alicia, whom Sloan handed up to him.

They said goodbye to the Sloans and their people, who would be traveling west and, hopefully, taking the posse with them — at least for a little while.

As they rode away from the camp Alicia said, "They were nice."

"They were real nice people."

She craned her neck to look at him.

"But I wouldn't want to live with them, Lancaster," she said, then looked forward again.

How the hell did she know he'd been thinking about that?

Chapter Seventeen

"What's wrong?" Aaron Delaware asked.

No one answered him.

Fred Brown was on the ground, walking around what had obviously been a large campsite with several campfires.

The others — Delaware, Sheriff Mathis, Tom Sullivan, and the posse members — were all mounted, watching Brown stalk about the ground, searching for sign.

"What is going on? Will someone tell me?"

Mathis remained silent. Delaware was paying both Brown and Sullivan, so he let Sullivan fill him in.

"Lancaster has finally decided to get smart," Sullivan said without looking at his employer.

"And what does that mean?" Delaware demanded.

"It means he rode his horse right into the middle of a large campsite," Sullivan said. "Lots of people, lots of other horses. He figured to lose his tracks in amongst them."

"Are we going to be able to find him?"

Sullivan almost smiled as he said, "Fred will find 'im."

After twenty minutes Delaware started to fidget in his saddle.

"Get down and stretch your legs," Sheriff Mathis said. "This could take a while."

"A while?" Delaware demanded as Mathis dismounted. "It's already taken a while."

Sullivan dismounted, and then the other men did, as well. Finally, Delaware stepped down. He rode regularly back east, but not over terrain like this. His butt was killing him, but he wouldn't let any of these men know it.

Mathis walked onto the campsite, careful to keep to the areas that Brown had already examined. He knew Brown was a better tracker than he was, but he started looking around just to give him something to do.

Eric Gates came up behind Mathis.

"How far are we gonna take this, Sheriff?" he asked.

Mathis turned and faced the man. Beyond Gates he could see the other two town merchants who, along with Delaware and his two men, made up the posse. They were Henry Taggert and Ben Ford.

"You askin' for all three, Eric?" Mathis asked.

"Dan," Gates said, "we got businesses waiting back home."

"This man has lost his daughter, Eric."

"And he's paying those two fellas to find her," Gates said. "They don't need us, Dan."

"They need me to make it official," Mathis said.

"Well then, they don't need the three of us," Gates said. "Let us go back."

"I can't, Eric."

"Why not?"

Mathis looked around.

"Something happened here, I'm not sure what, but I've got the uncomfortable feeling that we may have to split up soon. I'll need to go wherever Delaware and his men go. I've got to keep an eye on them."

"And us?"

"You're all duly sworn in as posse members," Mathis said, "and you're board members. This is part of your responsibility to the town."

"To the mayor, you mean."

"Right now," Mathis said, "the mayor and the town are the same thing. I'm sorry, but you've got to stay."

Gates scowled and walked back to Ford and Taggert to inform them of their obligation.

Mathis turned and looked at Fred Brown, who was down on one knee examining the ground. His demeanor told the lawman that he had found something. Behind him stood Tom Sullivan, and the two men were talking. Mathis walked over to them.

"What have you got?" he asked.

Brown looked at the sheriff over his shoulder, then at Sullivan, then back at the ground.

"He found Lancaster's horse," Sullivan said.

"Are you sure?"

"Left rear hoof's got a mark on it," Brown said. "Makes it distinctive."

Brown stood up.

"Which way did it go?"

"The tracks move off with the rest of them," Brown said.

"You mean Lancaster's riding with them now?"

"Looks that way."

"What's your problem, then?"

Brown looked at him, but it was Sullivan who spoke. Mathis had the feeling that these two knew each other so well that they never had to decide who was going to speak and who wasn't, they just knew.

"Who says I got a problem?"

"Come on, boys," Mathis said. "Talk to

me. I am in charge here . . . supposedly."

"He found the horse," Sullivan said, "but how do we know he's still riding it?"

"Come again?" Mathis said. "Are you saying he and the girl are on foot?"

"No," Sullivan said. "There were a lot of horses here. They could have switched. There are tracks of another horse that continue north. It could be them."

Mathis thought a moment, rubbing the back of his neck hard. "Okay, good point."

"So what do we do?" Brown asked.

"It's getting late," Mathis said. "I suggest we camp here for the night and talk it over."

"Suggest?" Sullivan asked.

Mathis frowned at himself and said, "We'll make camp here."

"I'll tell the others," Brown said.

"You do that."

As Brown and Sullivan went to talk to the others, Mathis looked down at the ground. Lancaster would be this smart, he thought. Switching horses while in this large camp was a good play. Riding along with them would have been a good play, also. There was no way Brown, as good a tracker as he was, would be able to tell for sure if Lancaster did switch. At least part of the posse was going to have to continue to follow the tracks of the group.

Chapter Eighteen

Lancaster and Alicia camped that night in Oklahoma. They had just crossed over from Texas as it was getting dark.

"I'm tired," Alicia said as they sat around the fire finishing their dinner. Lancaster had heated some of the stew that Rebecca Sloan had given them.

"I know, honey," he said. "So am I."

"But you do this all the time."

He smiled.

"I used to do it all the time," he said. "Not so much lately."

She yawned and asked, "Why not? Don't you like riding a horse anymore?"

"I do," he said. "I like riding a horse very much."

"Then why did you stop?"

"It's . . . complicated."

"Grown-up stuff?"

"Yes," he said, "grown-up stuff."

Her eyes drooped, then she jerked them wide, but they dropped again.

"Besides," he said, "you're ready to go

to sleep."

"Am not," she said sleepily. "I just ache."

"And you're sleepy," he said.

This time she didn't argue.

He laid her down and covered her with a blanket.

"What are we going to do tomorrow, Lancaster?" she asked.

"Well, we're going to find someplace to get you a bath."

"That sounds good," she said, and fell asleep.

It sounded good to him, too. He also needed to get some new clothes for both of them. It was time he cleaned up. He didn't want to look like a drunk when they reached Big Bend.

Of course, that wouldn't be for a while yet. Maybe by then he would have also put on some weight. And then there was the question of eluding the posse that was surely on their trail by now.

Lancaster took his gun out and checked it carefully. It hadn't been fired in over six months. It could use a cleaning, and so could his Winchester. He'd take care of that, too, when they stopped for a bath.

Despite the fact that they had switched horses, he knew he was going to have to take some other evasive action, as well. The best-case scenario would have the posse following the Sloan party for a while before realizing they'd been tricked. On the other hand, there might be someone with them who'd figure it out, and they'd continue north. Maybe the most he could hope for was to have caused some confusion, and maybe split the posse into two groups.

He'd lived in Dunworthy for six months, and in that time he had come to know the makeup of its people. His best guess told him that Sheriff Dan Mathis would come up with only two or three men for a posse. He wondered if Alicia's father, Aaron Delaware, was the type of man who would demand to ride along, maybe even bring a couple of men of his own. With that in mind, Lancaster figured there was a six- or seven-man posse on his heels. If it split in two, that would leave three or four men on his trail.

There were ways to split them up, as well.

Lancaster holstered his gun and looked up at the star-filled night sky. Being on the trail again was good. Having a purpose in life again was good, too. He didn't know how the little girl's mother in Big Bend would react to his proposition. It certainly wouldn't lessen the guilt he felt, but if she accepted maybe it would enable him to live with it a little better.

Maybe he could even crawl out of the bottle and start living again.

Still in Texas, Mathis and the posse were camped for the night, and broken into four parts. Mathis and Delaware were each sitting off on their own, while the three townsmen were sitting together. Brown and Sullivan sat side by side.

They ate that way until Mathis collected all the tin plates and brought them to the fire.

"Coffee's ready," he called out, having made a second pot. "I think we should gather around the fire and talk while we have it."

Nobody got up right away, but finally Brown and Sullivan came to the fire, followed by Gates, Taggert and Ford, and finally Aaron Delaware. From the pained look on his face Mathis figured that Delaware was having some problem getting up and down.

"Brown, here, has some doubts about what went on here a couple of days ago."

"A couple of days?" Delaware asked. "I thought we were a day behind them?"

"A day or two," Sullivan said. "It's hard to be sure."

"This camp is cold," Brown said. "They

left here at least two days ago."

"And was Lancaster with them?" Delaware asked.

"Sullivan has some thoughts on that," Mathis said. "Tell him."

Sullivan related to Delaware the same opinions he'd voiced to the sheriff earlier.

"So what you're saying," Delaware said when he was finished, "is that you don't know which way Lancaster went."

"There is no way to *know* which way he went," Brown replied.

"What the hell am I paying you men for?" Delaware demanded. "This man Lancaster has something that belongs to me, and I want it back. It's your job to find him. I don't need any more excuses." He stood up and looked down his nose at all of them. "I'm turning in. In the morning I'll expect you to tell me which way we're heading."

"Is any amount of money worth working for that man?" Eric Gates asked out loud when Delaware had left.

Brown looked at him and said, "Yes."

He and Sullivan took their coffee and went back to where they were sitting earlier, near their saddles.

"Sheriff, what's gonna happen when we find Lancaster?" Ford asked.

"I guess that's when we'll find out what

those two are really getting paid for."

"You're not gonna expect us to go up against them if they want to kill Lancaster, are you?" Taggert asked. "Because if you are, I can tell you right now —"

"Forget it, Taggert," Mathis said. "We'll be splitting up in the morning anyway."

"Splitting up . . . how?" Gates asked.

"You three will follow the trail west," Mathis said. "I'll go with Delaware and his men and continue north."

"Who do you think is gonna find Lancaster?" Ford asked.

"I think you three will catch up with whatever group of people were camped here, and you'll probably find Lancaster's horse. If that happens just double back and try to catch up with us."

"And what if we find Lancaster and the girl?" Gates asked. "What do we do then?"

"Lancaster was a gunman before he came to our town trying to drink himself to death," Taggert said. "He's probably still better with a gun than the three of us."

"If you find him," Mathis said, "talk to him, try to get him to come back. Don't brace him. I don't want any of you getting killed — but to tell you the truth, I don't think you'll find him."

All three men looked relieved.

"I think he was smart enough to switch horses, figuring he'd at least get us to split up."

"Then why are we?" Ford asked. "Why don't we just stay together?"

"Because," Mathis said, "there's always the chance that I'm wrong, or that Brown is wrong. We have to cover it both ways."

Mathis tossed the remnants of his coffee into the fire, causing it to flare up.

"Turn in, men," he said. "We're gonna get an early start in the morning."

The next morning they were all mounted up, the three possemen lined up opposite Mathis, Delaware, Brown and Sullivan. The three of them sat there, miserably listening to Mathis give them their instructions one final time.

"If you find him, reason with him," Mathis said. "He'll talk with you."

"What if he shoots at us?" Ford asked.

"He won't," Mathis said, "unless you give him reason to."

The three of them exchanged unhappy glances, then looked back at Mathis.

"If you catch up to the group and he's not with them, double back and come after us."

"Why can't we just head back to town?" Taggert asked.

"Because I'm telling you not to," Mathis said. "While you're a member of this posse you're under my command. Got it?"

They all nodded.

"Now get going," Mathis said.

"We ain't none of us trackers," Gates said. "What if we lose the trail?"

"You won't," Brown said. "There's several wagons and about twenty horses. Even you can't lose a trail like that. Trust me."

Finally, they turned their horses and rode away.

"You're putting a lot of faith in those three idiots," Aaron Delaware complained.

Mathis just looked at him.

"He's puttin' a lot of faith in the assumption they won't find him," Brown said, looking at Delaware, "and I agree. Lancaster's still riding north."

"Then let's get after him," Delaware said.

"I'm still heading this posse, Mr. Delaware," Mathis said.

"Fine," Delaware said. "What's our next move?"

Mathis stared at Delaware for a few moments, then said, "Let's get after him."

As he wheeled his horse around he thought he saw Fred Brown smile.

Chapter Nineteen

When Lancaster spotted the town of Tunica, Oklahoma, he knew it was the right one. It was small, slightly run-down, and there were no telegraph wires running into it. It had a hotel, a saloon, and, he knew, somewhere it would have a bathtub.

He rode up to the livery stable, dismounted, and helped Alicia down. A man came walking out, a big man with a leather apron and a dirty face, wiping his hands on a rag. Blacksmith, Lancaster thought, and liveryman.

"Help ya?"

"We need to put the horse up for one night."

"No problem."

"Feed him, rub him down —"

"I know how to handle a horse, mister," the man said, cutting him off.

"How much do I owe you?"

The man waved a hand and said, "Pay when you leave. I got work to do."

He started walking the horse into the

livery, and Lancaster hurriedly removed his rifle and their supply sack from the saddle.

"What do we do now, Lancaster?" Alicia asked, looking up at him.

"We find you a bathtub."

"Sounds good to me," she said, crossing her arms over her chest.

Lancaster couldn't exactly remember when he started liking her as a person, but looking down at her now he knew that he did.

They walked to the hotel.

"That your kid?" the clerk asked.

"That's right. What of it?" Lancaster asked. "Don't you allow kids?"

"I just don't want no funny stuff in my hotel," the man said.

Lancaster paused in the act of writing his name in the register and stared at the man. He was in his forties, very thin, with a long neck that would fit in two clenched hands.

"I, uh, just meant . . ." he said, trailing off and looking away from Lancaster's stare.

Lancaster finished registering and accepted the key from the man.

"You got bathtubs here?"

"No, sir."

"Is there a bathhouse?"

"No."

"What about a barbershop with a bathtub?"

"No, sir."

"Is there a bathtub in town?"

"Yes, sir."

"Well, where is it?"

"It's at Miss Marion's . . . down the street."

"Miss Marion's?" Lancaster asked. "What's that? A boardinghouse?"

The clerk looked at Alicia nervously, then back at Lancaster.

"Sort of."

"Okay," Lancaster said to Alicia, "we'll take our things upstairs and then we're going to Miss Marion's."

"For a bath," Alicia said. "Yay! I need one."

"You know what?" Lancaster said. "So do I."

"Yes," Alicia said, making a face, "you do."

After stowing their gear in the room — Lancaster left his rifle there along with the supply sack, because carrying a rifle would attract too much attention — they left the hotel and walked down the street until they came to a sign that said MISS MARION'S.

"This looks like the place," Lancaster said.

Chapter Twenty

Lancaster took one look around and knew immediately where they were. The woman who approached them was heavyset, in her fifties, all made up with a look on her face that was not very welcoming.

"Is that your daughter?"

Lancaster was so surprised, he almost forgot their story.

"Uh, yes, she is."

"You got a lot of nerve bringin' her in here," the woman said loudly. Her voice attracted the girls from the sitting room, and some of them came into the hall to see what was happening. They were all wearing filmy and revealing gowns, and Alicia's eyes widened as she saw them.

"Ma'am —" Lancaster started.

"I'm Miss Marion," the woman said, cutting him off, "and we don't take kindly to this kind of behavior. This little girl doesn't belong in this kind of place."

"Ma'am," he said again, "I didn't know what kind of place this was when I walked in. We just got to town, and I was looking for a bathtub."

"A what?"

"A bathtub," Lancaster said. "See, she — my daughter . . . Alicia — needs a bath."

Miss Marion looked down at Alicia's grubby hands and face, and her dirty clothes, and said, "You know, she needs a lot more than a bath."

"I know, ma'am," he said, "but I thought a bath was the place to start. I asked around town and they said that there was a tub at Miss Marion's — only nobody told me that Miss Marion's was a . . . a cathouse."

Miss Marion stared at him for a few moments, her head cocked to one side.

"You're telling the truth, aren't you?"

"Yes, ma'am," he said, "I am."

"Let the little girl use the bathtub, Marion," a dark-haired girl with pale skin and huge violet eyes said.

"Yeah," a tall, willowy blonde said, "she's a cute little thing. Let her take a bath."

"You'll have to pay for it," Miss Marion said to Lancaster.

"Yes, ma'am," he said. "I intended to."

"And she's too young to be in the tub by herself," Marion said. "I don't want no little girl drowning in one of my tubs."

"She won't drown, ma'am," he said, but

suddenly he realized that he was expected to bathe Alicia. He hadn't thought about that before.

"I'll help bathe her," the dark-haired girl with the violet eyes stepped forward and said. "It's early, and we ain't got much business."

"What do you know about bathing a child?" the blonde asked.

"I had three little sisters," the dark-haired girl said, "and I bathed every one of them."

"Do you want Amanda to help you?" Miss Marion asked Lancaster.

"I'd be obliged to both of you, ma'am," Lancaster said. "The girl's mother used to do it, but . . . but she's not with us anymore."

"You poor thing," Amanda said, coming up to Alicia and taking her hand. "You come along with me."

"You go along too, mister," Marion said. "I swear, now I'm rentin' out bathtubs to kids."

Lancaster fell in behind Amanda and Alicia. The little girl was searching high and low, and finally turned to look at Lancaster.

"I don't see any cats," she said.

Amanda laughed, and Lancaster thought his face must have turned red.

Chapter Twenty-one

Apparently Amanda had told the truth. She was very natural with Alicia, talking to her the whole time, filling the tub, letting her test the water, undressing her, and getting her into the water. At one point Amanda glanced over at Lancaster, who was looking the other way.

"Are you embarrassed to see your own daughter naked?" she asked.

"Uh . . . ," he said, not sure how to answer that question.

Amanda laughed and said, "That's sweet."

"This feels really good," Alicia said as the warm water soaked into her skin and washed away the grime and dust.

"What about you, Poppa?" Amanda asked.

"What about me?"

"Do you want a bath, too?"

He hesitated, then said, "I was thinking about it, yeah, but I don't want to get Miss Marion all upset."

"She won't get upset," Amanda said. "You stay here with Alicia and make sure she doesn't drown. I'll arrange a bath for you."

"I appreciate that," Lancaster said.

Amanda smiled and headed for the door, then stopped and asked, "What do you like?"

"Uh, what do you mean?"

"Blondes, redheads —"

"Blondes, uh, I guess . . ."

"You got it," she said, and left the room.

"Lancaster?" Alicia said.

"Yes?"

"You can look if you want," she said. "I'm all covered with soapy water."

Lancaster looked over at her, then moved closer to the tub, remembering what Miss Marion and Amanda had said about her drowning.

"See?" she said. "Can't see anything."

He could see her wet face and wet hair, and occasionally a knee or a foot, wet and slippery.

"It looks really good," he said.

"It is," Alicia said. "You'll see when Amanda gives you your bath."

"Uh, yeah . . ."

"Lancaster?"

"Yeah?"

"Do I have to keep calling you Lancaster?"

"I guess so."

"You won't tell me your first name?"

"No."

"Please?"

"No," he said. "Not yet."

"When?"

"I don't know," he said. "Later."

"Well, then, are we gonna buy some new clothes?"

"Yes."

"Good," she said, "I want a new dress."

"You need a new dress," he said, "and maybe some trousers."

"They're for boys."

"Out here girls wear 'em too," he told her. "It's easier to ride."

She frowned, thinking about it, then said, "Well, the saddle does hurt my legs some. Can we go and buy the clothes right after our baths?" she asked.

"Sure."

"And then something to eat?"

"Yes," he said, "and then a good night's sleep in a real bed." At that moment he realized that he'd gotten one room, with one bed. Well, they would deal with that when they came to it.

"And then what?" she asked.

"And then back on the trail tomorrow," he said. "We've got to stay ahead of that posse."

"You still think there's a posse?"

"Oh, yeah," he said, "I'm sure of it."

"Even after we changed horses?"

"The posse is bound to have somebody who'll figure out what we did," he said. "Your daddy probably used his money to hire the best tracker he could find."

"What can we do to keep them from catching up to us?"

"Well," he said, "there are a lot of ways to try to throw somebody off a scent. We're just going to have to try some tricks and see how good this tracker is."

"I don't think he'll be better than you," she said, playing with the soap.

"I guess we'll just have to see," he said, "won't we?"

"I guess we will."

At that point the door opened and Amanda stepped in. With her was the tall, willowy blonde.

"Okay, Poppa," Amanda said, "Teresa will take you to your bath."

"Uh, okay," he said. He looked at Alicia. "Don't give Amanda any trouble."

"I won't."

"Of course she won't," Amanda said.

"We're friends, aren't we, Alicia?"

"Yup."

As Lancaster stepped past Amanda and Teresa took his arm, the dark-haired girl said, "And don't you give Teresa any trouble either, you hear?"

Chapter Twenty-two

Teresa linked her arm through Lancaster's and walked him down the hall. Her shoulder was pressing against his, as was her hip. He could feel the heat of her skin, and her perfume made him light-headed. It had been a long time since he'd had a woman, and he was wondering if she was going to try to give him more than a bath. He didn't think he was quite ready for that.

They walked to a door, which she opened, and then stepped into a room with a steaming bathtub.

"You struck me as a man who would like hot water," she said, closing the door behind them.

"The hotter the better."

"Good," she said, smiling, "I like hot water too."

She was tall and slender, but she was wearing some kind of undergarment that pushed her breasts together and up. Her cleavage was pale and scented. She reached behind her back to undo herself.

"Whoa, wait —" he said.

She froze.

"What is it?"

"I . . . I just wanted to take a bath, ma'am."

She stared at him, blinking several times as if she didn't understand.

"You mean . . . by yourself?"

"Yes, ma'am," he said.

"Don't you like . . . women?"

"Oh, it's nothing like that, ma'am," he said. "You're very beautiful, and under other circumstances I'd be only too happy to take a bath with you, but . . . the truth of it is I . . . I been sick, and I'm afraid I wouldn't be much . . . fun for you."

"Fun?" she asked.

"Well . . . maybe it would just be too much hard work for you," he said, thinking that the word "fun" might have offended her. "I don't know what you call what you do, ma'am, fun or work, but I do know that I only want a bath . . . if that's all right."

She dropped her arms to her side and all sign of flirtatiousness was gone.

"Hey," she said, "that's fine with me. Do you want me to stay or leave?"

"Oh," Lancaster said, "I'd much rather do this alone, ma'am."

"Okay, cowboy," she said, "and stop

calling me 'ma'am,' okay? My name is just Teresa — or Terry."

"Okay, Miss Teresa —"

"No," she said, "not *Miss* Teresa, just Teresa. Look, I'll give you fifteen minutes for a quick bath and then I've got to have the room back, all right?"

"That's fine, ma'— Teresa. Thank you."

"Sure," she said, but she hesitated before leaving. "That's a real cute kid you got there, mister."

"Thank you," he said. "I think so too."

"Where you headed with her?"

"Kansas."

"That where her mother is?"

"Her mother's dead."

"Oh," Teresa said. "Tough break."

"Yeah."

"Lost my mother when I was a kid too," she said with her hand on the doorknob. "My father, too. She's lucky she's got you."

"Thank you."

"Well, okay," Teresa said, opening the door, "I'll be back in fifteen minutes — maybe twenty. Why don't we make it twenty?"

"I don't want to get you in trouble with your boss."

"I can handle her," Teresa said. "Twenty minutes, okay?"

"Twenty it is," Lancaster said. "Much obliged."

"Sure," she said, and left.

Lancaster let out a sigh of relief. He just didn't know if he'd be able to perform with a woman right now, and would rather have just avoided the embarrassment.

He got undressed, pulled a chair over by the tub so he could lay his gun on it, and got into the bathtub.

True to her word, Teresa returned in twenty minutes.

She found Lancaster dressed and damp.

"Not enough towels?" she asked.

"I, uh, dozed off and had to get dressed real fast before you, uh, got here."

"You coulda taken the time to dry off," she said, shaking her head. "Well, come on. Your kid is waitin' out front."

He followed her down the hall again, this time all the way to the front foyer. Alicia wasn't there, though, she was in the sitting room with the other women, who were making a fuss over her. She looked real clean, even more so compared to the dirty dress she was wearing.

"There's your daddy," one girl said.

"Hey, daddy, you gonna buy this little girl a new dress?" another asked.

"I sure am," he said. "Come on, honey. We've taken up enough of these nice, uh, people's time." He put his hand out, and she ran up to him and took it.

" 'Bye," she said, waving to all the girls with her other hand.

Lancaster tugged her into the foyer, where Miss Marion and Amanda were waiting. Amanda went down on one knee to give Alicia a hug.

"Ma'am," Lancaster said to Miss Marion, "I'm truly obliged for the use of your bathtubs. How much do I owe you?"

"Forget it," Marion said with a wave of her hand. "Maybe you'll come later by yourself and spend some money, huh?"

"Maybe, ma'am," Lancaster said. "Thank you."

"You buy that little girl a nice new dress, you hear?" the older woman said.

"Yes, ma'am."

"Do you need any help buyin' it?" Amanda asked.

"No," Lancaster said, "but thanks anyway."

"Well," she said, "if you change your mind, you know where I am."

Lancaster and Alicia went out the front door and stood out front for a moment, getting their bearings.

"When are you going to come back here and spend money?" Alicia asked.

"Never mind," Lancaster said, "let's go and see where we can get us some new clothes."

Chapter Twenty-three

The only place in town that sold clothing was the general store. Going in, Lancaster doubted they'd have much of a selection.

"I got boys," the owner said.

"Will they fit her?" Lancaster asked.

"Might be a little baggy," the man said. "I got a girl of my own, and she wears 'em." The owner — who was also the clerk — was a man in his thirties. Lancaster wasn't sure if he was telling the truth or just trying to sell some pants.

"If you need help shopping for her," the man said, "I can have my missus come down."

"I think I can buy some clothes," Lancaster said, "but thanks. Come on, Alicia."

"I have to wear boys' pants?" she asked.

"Just when we're riding," he said. "They'll protect your legs."

"What about a dress?"

"We're going to look right now."

There was a rack of dresses in the back, and he and Alicia walked up to it. Most of them were for women, but he found a few that were smaller.

"Can I help you?"

Lancaster turned at the sound of a woman's voice. She was handsome, and he assumed she was the owner's wife.

"Uh, I was looking for a dress, ma'am, for a little — uh, for my daughter?"

"We just have a few out here, but I have some more in the back. What kind were you interested in?"

"What . . . kind?"

"A party dress? A day dress? Something for a special occasion?"

"Uh, no, ma'am, just something to, uh, wear."

"A day dress."

"I guess."

"Well, it'll be getting hot soon, so I assume you'll want something in cotton?"

"Uh, I guess so."

"Something plain? Or with a pattern? Gingham, perhaps?" she asked.

Lancaster cursed the store owner for sending his wife over to ask him questions he couldn't answer. He would have preferred to just take something off the rack.

"Is this the first time you're doing this?" she asked him.

"I suppose it shows," he said.

"Why don't I take the little girl in the back and see what I have?" she suggested. "What's your name?"

"Alicia."

"Alicia, would you like to come and look at some dresses with me?"

"Yes, ma'am."

"All right, then," the woman said, putting out her hand.

"He's not very good at buying dresses . . . ," Lancaster heard Alicia saying as she and the woman walked away.

"Men never are, dear."

While Alicia was with the store owner's wife Lancaster collected his other purchases, including some supplies, a pair of new jeans for himself, two new shirts, and a pair of boys' pants for Alicia.

After about a half hour the woman and Alicia came back out. Lancaster had already paid for everything else and was trying to avoid the owner's small talk by staring out the window.

"Here we are," the woman announced.

Lancaster turned and looked down at Alicia, who was wearing a dress that was mostly blue, in some sort of pattern he wasn't sure about.

"It's gingham," Alicia said.

"Ah . . ."

"Can I have it, Lancaster?"

"Do you want it?" He crouched down to ask her the question.

"Oh, yes."

"Then of course you can have it." He stood up. "Thank you," he said to the woman.

"You're quite welcome." She was looking at him funny, though, as if something bothered her.

He went to the counter to settle with the owner. As he was standing there counting out the money for the dress, Alicia came alongside him, looked longingly at a jar of licorice, then looked up at him with "that" face.

"And some licorice," he said. Smiling widely, she stuck her hand in the jar.

They left the general store with Alicia wearing her new dress and chewing on one of the licorice sticks, Lancaster carrying their purchases under his left arm. He held her hand with his right and they walked back toward the hotel.

"We'll leave all our things at the hotel and go get something to eat," he said.

"All right."

They went up to the room, dropped off their things, and he changed into his new clothes. There was one awkward moment, but they just turned their backs to each other.

"Should I throw this away?" she asked, holding the licorice up as they walked back down the stairs to the lobby.

"No, why?"

"It might ruin my dinner."

"Are you enjoying it?"

"Oh, yes."

"Then finish it," he said. "If you don't finish your dinner, we'll just take it back to the room with us."

"Lancaster," she said, squeezing his hand, "you're a very wonderful man."

He'd never been called that before, and having her do it made him feel something in his chest — like a lump.

"Thank you, Alicia."

Chapter Twenty-four

They found a small café, where they sat at a table for the first time and had a meal together. Lancaster was very impressed with Alicia's table manners and her ability to order what she wanted to eat without a fuss. He thought all children were a problem in restaurants. At least, all the children he'd ever seen sitting at other tables with their parents were. As if to illustrate that fact, there was a little boy about her age at another table who was complaining about having to eat his vegetables.

"How do you feel about vegetables?" Lancaster asked her.

She smiled and said, "I love them."

"You're a very wonderful child, did you know that, Alicia?"

"Thank you, Lancaster."

While they were eating a man entered the café, stopped just inside the front door, and looked around. Lancaster noticed that he was wearing a sheriff's badge. If there had been a telegraph office in town, he would have worried that someone might have wired his description, along with Alicia's. As it was, he just sat tight and calmly waited to see what the man was going to do.

Finally, he approached their table.

"Remember, Alicia," he said quickly, "I'm your daddy."

"Yes, Lanc— I mean, Daddy."

The sheriff, a man of medium height but thickly built, stopped right next to their table.

"Sir? Could I have a word with you?"

"Of course, Sheriff," Lancaster said. "What's the problem?"

"I'm Sheriff Wilkins. Is your name Lancaster?"

"Yes, it is."

"Mr. Lancaster, could we step away from the table, please?"

"I don't like to leave my daughter alone —"

"We'll be able to see her from the other side of the room." The sheriff looked at Alicia. "Honey, we're just going over there. Will you be all right?"

"Yes, sir," Alicia said, her fork in her hand. "I'll just be eating my vegetables."

"There's a good girl," Sheriff Wilkins said. He looked at Lancaster. "Sir?"

"Sure," Lancaster said, taking his napkin

from his lap and putting it on the table. "I'll be right back, honey."

Alicia nodded with a mouthful of vegetables.

Lancaster stood up and followed the sheriff to the other side of the room.

"What's this all about, Sheriff?"

"I just have some questions, is all," Sheriff Wilkins said. "Is that little girl your daughter?"

"Yes, she is."

"Can you prove it?"

Lancaster contrived to look put upon, like a father who's having his paternity questioned.

"Do I have to prove it?" he asked. "And if so, why?"

"Sir," Wilkins said, "I'm just asking questions —"

"Yes, I know you are, Sheriff. What I'd like to know is why you're asking them."

"Now, don't get upset —"

"I am getting upset, Sheriff," Lancaster said, "I'm getting very upset. Who is questioning whether or not I am my daughter's father?"

"No one's actually questioning it," Wilkins said. "Look, you were in the general store a little while ago buying a dress."

"So?"

"So, you weren't very good at it," Wilkins

150

said. "Your daughter appears to be about seven —"

"Eight."

"All right, eight, and you're buying her a dress like it's the first time."

"It *was* the first time, for Chrissake," Lancaster said, getting into his part so well that his heart was actually starting to pound. He *felt* like Alicia's father. "Her dead mother used to do it, God rest her soul —"

"I'm sorry, sir," Wilkins said, "I didn't know —"

"And what else prompted this?" Lancaster asked. "This is because of the lady in the general store, isn't it? The one who helped with the dress?"

"She said the little girl called you Lancaster," Wilkins said, "and not Daddy."

"It's a phase she's going through," Lancaster said. "Do you have children?"

"No, sir, I don't."

"Well, then, take my word for it, Sheriff, they go through phases."

"I'm sure they do."

"Is there anything else you need explained?"

Looking chagrined, the sheriff said, "No, I don't think so, sir. Thanks for your time."

"I'll go back to my dinner now."

"Yes, sir."

The sheriff left, and Lancaster walked back to the table and sat down. He was still breathing hard.

"What's wrong?"

"Nothing," he said. "The sheriff just had some questions."

"About me?"

"About you and me."

"Is everything all right?"

He looked directly at her and said, "Everything is fine, sweetie. Finish your dinner."

After a moment she put her fork down and said, "Lancaster?"

"Yes?"

"I don't have anyone but you, you know."

He took his eyes from his plate and looked at her. He knew exactly what her point was. If he didn't talk to her, who would?

He explained that the woman in the store had some doubts about him really being her father, and she had talked to the sheriff about them. The sheriff had, in turn, come to question him.

"Did I say something wrong?" she asked.

"I don't think so, honey. Did you? What did you and the lady talk about in the back room?"

"Just dresses."

"Then I don't think you said anything wrong."

"Then why would she —"

"I wasn't very good at buying you a dress, remember?"

"She said all men were like that."

"Well, I guess she expected a man with a daughter to be a little better at it. I guess I'm just not very good at being a father."

"Yes," Alicia said, "you are. Lancaster, you're better at it than my real daddy is."

He got that lump in his chest again. It wasn't anything he'd ever experienced before meeting Alicia Delaware.

"Thank you, honey," he said. "Now, why don't we finish our dinner? You want some pie after that?"

"Yes, please," she said. "Peach."

Chapter Twenty-five

The incident with Sheriff Wilkins worried Lancaster. If the posse got this far Sheriff Wilkins was sure to remember them, but there was nothing Lancaster could do about that.

He wondered why the woman in the general store had taken it upon herself to talk to the law. Did he seem so unlikely a father figure that the woman was afraid Alicia was in danger? What would she tell Sheriff Mathis if he arrived in town and questioned her? Would she say Alicia seemed frightened, or seemed as if she were being held by force?

After dinner they walked around town, Lancaster looking for either a gunsmith shop or a hardware store where they might clean weapons. Finding none, he decided he'd have to clean his own weapons that night.

When they got back to the room Lancaster addressed the business of sleeping arrangements.

"You can have the bed, Alicia," he said. "I'll bunk on the floor."

"Why?" she asked.

"Well . . ."

"I'm very small, Lancaster," she said. "Small for my age. I don't take up much room. We can both sleep in the bed."

"You wouldn't mind?"

"No," she said, shaking her head, her face very serious. "I think I'd feel safer if you slept close by me."

"All right, then," he said, "I'll stay right here."

She went to bed first, though, and he tucked her in on one side.

"My momma used to kiss me goodnight when she tucked me in."

"Is that so."

To his own surprise, he leaned down and kissed her warm forehead. Maybe he wasn't so bad at this father business, after all.

Lancaster had been thinking about leaving the room while she was asleep, but he thought better of it. It might frighten her to wake and find him gone. Also, he'd probably end up at the saloon, and once there he didn't know if he'd be able to resist taking a drink.

He moved a chair over to the window and looked down at the street while he cleaned his Peacemaker and his Winchester. He thought about the Walker Colt, which had always been his backup gun. They'd been in such a hurry to leave that he'd left it in Dunworthy.

It wasn't very late, but this town looked as if it went to sleep early. The window was open a notch, and he noticed that he couldn't hear a thing, no laughter or voices from a saloon. In a quiet town like this his appearance with a child would stand out in people's minds — especially the women at the whorehouse, the couple in the general store, and the sheriff.

When they left Tunica he was definitely going to have to start taking more evasive action.

She visited him again that night.

It was odd, because he hadn't seen or heard from her since he'd first seen Alicia. It was as if this little girl had already taken the place of . . . that little girl. But tonight she was there, in his dreams, and he woke with a start and sat straight up in bed.

"Are you all right?" Alicia asked.

"Hmm?" It took him a moment to realize where he was, and who she was. He had stretched out on top of the quilt, next to Alicia, only an hour before. "Oh, I'm sorry. Did I scare you?"

"No," she said. "Are you scared? Did you have a very bad dream?"

"Yes," he said. "Yes, it was a very bad dream."

She sat up next to him and looked up at him. There was enough moonlight coming through the window to illuminate the room.

"My momma always told me it helped to talk about bad dreams."

"Oh, not this one, I don't think," he said to her.

"Was it that scary?"

He looked down at her and ran one hand over his damp face.

"Yes," he said, "it was *very* scary. I wouldn't want to tell it to you and then have you dream it. You wouldn't like that, would you?"

"No," she said, shaking her head. "I wouldn't want to have a grown-up person's bad dream."

He laughed and put his arm around her shoulders.

"I'm not so sure about that, Alicia," he said. "You're already smarter than a lot of grown-ups I know."

In the morning they had a quick breakfast in the same café they'd eaten at the night before. After they were finished they walked to the livery, Lancaster carrying his Winchester and their supply sack, which was much fuller than it had been when they first arrived.

The same man who had taken the horse the day before brought it out. He told Lancaster how much he owed and accepted the money.

"I got work to do," he said, and went back inside.

Lancaster thought that this was probably the only person they'd encountered in town who wouldn't remember them.

Chapter Twenty-six

Two days later, everything Lancaster had been worrying about came true.

Sheriff Mathis, Aaron Delaware, Brown, and Sullivan rode into Tunica and stopped at the livery.

"We're lookin' for a man and a little girl," Mathis said to the man. "Did they come through here?"

"I got a lot of work to do," the man said. "You puttin' up your horses?"

"Don't know yet," Mathis said. "Did you see 'em?"

"I didn't see nothin'," the man said. "I'm too busy. You wanna put your horses up, you come back."

With that the big man turned and went back inside.

"Maybe you're wrong," Delaware said to Brown.

Brown didn't dignify the remark with an answer.

"I'll talk to the local sheriff," Mathis said. "You three go to the saloon or something."

"You think Lancaster would take her to a saloon?" Delaware asked.

"He just means," Brown said, "for us to go to the saloon and wait for him."

"Oh."

They rode into town, then split up. Delaware, Sullivan, and Brown stopped their horses in front of the saloon, while Mathis rode on until he found the sheriff's office.

"Son of a bitch!" Sheriff Jerry Wilkins swore.

"What?" Mathis asked.

"Mrs. Atkins, the woman at the general store, she said something didn't seem right about those two."

"They were at the general store?"

Wilkins nodded, drumming the fingers of his right hand on his desk. Mathis, standing in front of the man's desk, found it annoying.

"Yeah, they bought some supplies, and the man got the little girl a dress. That's what made Mrs. Atkins get suspicious. He didn't know what he was doing."

"And he passed the girl off as his daughter?"

"Yep," Wilkins said, "lied about that right out."

Mathis took the time to describe Lancaster to his counterpart, and Wilkins said,

"That's him, all right." This was the first real indication Mathis had that they really were chasing Lancaster, and that he had the little girl with him.

"Much obliged for your help, Sheriff."

"Sorry I didn't do more when they were here," Wilkins said, "but there was no way for me to know for sure that he wasn't the little girl's father."

"I know that," Mathis said, "especially if she was backing his story."

"There's one more thing."

"What?"

"Both of them bathed."

"What's the significance of that?"

"There's only one place in this town that's got bathtubs."

"Where's that?"

"The whorehouse."

Mathis found Delaware, Sullivan, and Brown sitting at a back table with frosty mugs of beer. He licked his lips, got a mug for himself, and joined them. Brown was the man sitting with his back to the wall. Sullivan was sitting so he could see the front entrance.

"Well?" Delaware asked.

Mathis took his time savoring the first few swallows of cold beer.

"They were here, all right," he said, and gave them all the details.

"He must have threatened her to get her to back his story," Aaron Delaware said when the sheriff had finished.

Mathis looked at Delaware and said nothing. The man had steadfastly refused to believe, right from the beginning, that his daughter might have gone with Lancaster willingly, that she might not have wanted to see him at all.

"Sure, Mr. Delaware," Sullivan said to the man who was paying him, "that must be it."

"Where'd they go?" Delaware asked.

"The sheriff doesn't know," Mathis said, "but there are some other people in town who spoke to them. We can question them."

"I'll take the whorehouse," Brown said.

"I'll go with you," Mathis said. "Mr. Delaware, why don't you and Sullivan talk to the people at the general store?"

"A whorehouse!" Delaware spat out. "That madman took my daughter to a whorehouse? Who knows what pains she's suffered?"

"Well," Mathis said, "we know she took a bath."

Brown tried to keep a straight face.

"Sullivan," Mathis said, "why don't you do the talking when you get to the general store?"

"Sure."

"Why him?"

"Because he's not emotionally involved, Mr. Delaware."

"Are you saying I'm not in complete control of myself?" Delaware demanded.

"I don't think I said that at all," Mathis said. "I just suggested something I think would work better."

Somewhat mollified, Delaware said, "Well, okay."

Mathis finished his beer and said, "Let's do it. If we get finished quickly enough we can still get back on the trail today before nightfall."

"Sure would like to spend at least one night here," Sullivan said.

Mathis used his thumb and forefinger to wipe beer from the corners of his mouth.

"Might not be a bad idea, at that," he said.

"I disagree!" Delaware shouted. "The longer we spend here, the farther away they get."

"They spent one night here," Brown said. "If we do likewise we shouldn't lose any ground on them."

"The horses could use the rest," Mathis said. "Okay, then, we'll spend the night here and get an early start in the morning."

"I object!" Delaware said.

"I'll take your objection under consideration, Mr. Delaware. Let's get our horses taken care of before we run our errands, shall we?"

"I can do that," Brown said. "I'll walk 'em over there and meet you at the whorehouse. What's it called?"

"Miss Marion's."

"I guess we'll go right over to the general store," Sullivan said, standing. "Where should we meet?"

"Back here," Mathis said. "One hour."

The other three men nodded their agreement. Then they all left the saloon together and split up.

Chapter Twenty-seven

Mathis was the first one back to the saloon. He got himself a beer, and although the place was a little busier than before, he managed to get the same table.

Fred Brown had decided to interview one of the whores in more depth. He had chosen Amanda, the one who had bathed the child, Alicia. Mathis didn't know what was keeping Delaware and Sullivan, but they walked in within the next ten minutes, Sullivan shaking his head.

"What's the matter?" Mathis asked.

Sullivan sat at the table while Delaware went to the bar to see if they had any brandy.

"He offered to buy the general store from these people if they told him where Lancaster went."

"And?"

"They didn't know," Sullivan said. "They *said* they didn't know right at the beginning, but he kept on believing they did. Seems the woman took the little girl into the back to show her some dresses. Mr. Delaware there feels she must have learned something from Alicia."

"So did he buy the place?"

"No," Sullivan said.

Delaware returned and sat at the table.

"Can't even get a decent drink in this godforsaken country," he complained. "Why do you people insist on living out here?"

Mathis and Sullivan exchanged a glance, but each for their own reasons decided not to answer the question.

A saloon girl, a pretty little blond thing, came over and asked if they wanted anything.

"Bring three beers, will you, darlin'?" Sullivan asked.

"Sure, handsome."

Sullivan smiled. Of all the things in the world he was, handsome wasn't one of them.

"Where's Fred?" he asked. "As if I didn't know."

"One of the girls gave Alicia her bath," Mathis said. "Brown is . . . questioning her."

"Good," Delaware said, "at least someone here is working."

"He's workin', all right," Sullivan said.

"What did you find out, Sheriff?" Delaware asked.

"Nothin' you'd want to hear, Mr. Delaware."

"Don't tell me what I do or do not want to hear," Delaware insisted.

"Fine," Mathis said. "The, uh, lady who bathed the child said she seemed very 'fond' of her father, and very happy to be with him."

"Her father?" Delaware's face turned so red, Mathis thought it would explode.

"That's what she said."

Delaware had to try several times before he could form words.

"He's corrupted her mind!" he said, spitting the words out.

"You asked me what I found out," Mathis said. "That's what I found out. She also said that she and her 'father' looked adorable tog—"

"That's enough!" Delaware ordered. He leaned forward and said, "Sheriff Mathis, you're getting much too much pleasure out of this."

Mathis leaned toward the man. "Mr. Delaware, I'm not getting any pleasure at all from any of this." With that he stood, left his half-finished beer, and walked out.

Delaware looked at the face of Tom Sullivan.

"Mr. Sullivan," he said, "we're going to have to change the foundation of our agreement."

"Why do I get the feeling that you're gonna offer us more money?"

"A lot more money," Delaware said.

"In that case," Sullivan said, "you better wait until my partner gets here."

Mathis went to his hotel room, removed his boots and his gunbelt, and reclined on the bed. He hated posses, mostly because he missed his wife when he was away. This one he hated for even more reasons. He could not see giving that little girl back to Aaron Delaware. The man just did not strike him as fatherly, and he pitied the child if she were to be brought up by him alone. He was sworn to uphold the law, though, had always honored his oath, and he had certainly never tried to bend the law to his own will. As much as he would like to see Lancaster get away with the girl, it was his duty to track the man down and bring him back, even if he didn't like it.

Which he didn't.

"Do either of you have a problem with that?" Delaware asked Brown and Sullivan.

Brown had returned only minutes earlier,

and Delaware had outlined his new agreement with them. The two men exchanged a glance, then Brown asked, "What about the sheriff?"

"Since when has the law concerned you two?" Delaware asked with almost a sneer, and the next thing he knew his right wrist was captured by a viselike grip belonging to Tom Sullivan. For such a thin, almost frail-looking man he had surprising strength. Delaware tried not to show the pain on his face, but failed.

"Let me make something clear to you, Mr. Delaware," Brown said.

"I —"

"We'll work for you," Brown said, ignoring the man's attempt to speak. "We'll gladly take your money to get your daughter back and do whatever else you want done, but don't ever think that you know anything about us, about what we'd do or what we wouldn't do, about what concerns us and what doesn't concern us. Am I understood?"

Delaware nodded.

"You'll have to speak up," Brown said, "so that Tom can hear you, and then maybe he'll let go of your wrist."

"Y-yes," Delaware said, "I understand."

"Good."

Brown and Sullivan exchanged another glance, then Sullivan loosened his grip.

"The sheriff shouldn't be a problem," Brown said.

"Good," Delaware said, rubbing his wrist, "that's . . . that's very good."

"Now, I think you should go and get some rest, Mr. Delaware," Brown said. "We've still got a long way to ride, and I know the sheriff wants to get an early start."

"Yes," Delaware said, "yes, of course."

Delaware stood and left, already planning his revenge on these two men after they helped him get his revenge on Lancaster.

Chapter Twenty-eight

"How was the whore?" Sullivan asked his partner.

"She was fine," Brown said, "just fine. You should go over and see her before we leave town."

"I might just do that. What'd she tell you about Lancaster?"

"She said he looked sickly," Brown said. "He pleaded bein' sick when one of the whores tried to take a bath with him."

"Maybe he just doesn't like women."

"No," Brown said, "she said he liked 'em, all right. She guessed he just wasn't ready after bein' so sick and all."

"Well," Sullivan said, "I guess fallin' into a bottle qualifies as being sick."

Brown stared across the table at his partner. The two men had been born about as far apart as you could be. Sullivan had lived in the East when he was a child — New York then Philadelphia. When he came out west he met Brown, who had been born and raised in California. Sullivan was more educated than

Brown, and in fact was quite a reader. He also fancied himself something of a poet. Brown would always see his partner writing on scraps of paper when they were in a hotel room or camped on the trail, just the two of them, but he never talked about it, and he never asked Brown to read it. That suited Brown, who found reading a bore — maybe because he had such a hard time with it.

The partnership worked well, because each knew his place. Brown was the tracker, Sullivan was the thinker, but when it came to killing, they each took a turn. If it came down to killing Lancaster and the sheriff, they would split it up between them.

"He ain't drinkin'," Brown said, "unless he's carrying a bottle with him."

Sullivan looked at Brown, then at the bartender. He got up and walked to the bar.

"Two beers," he said.

"Comin' up."

When the man brought the drinks over Sullivan paid for them, leaving the change on the bar.

"I'm looking for a man and a little girl who rode in here about two days ago."

"Heard about it," the bartender said, "but didn't see them."

"Not even the man?"

"Nope."

"Didn't come in for a beer?"

"No."

"Any other saloons in town?"

"No."

"Anyplace else to get a drink?"

"Miss Marion's about the only other place I can think of."

"Any restaurants or cafés in town?"

"Some," the bartender said, "but they don't serve liquor."

"Much obliged," Sullivan said, walking back to the table.

"Lancaster drink anything at the whorehouse?" he asked his partner.

"No."

"Not here, either," Sullivan said. "I guess he's not drinking."

"He might have a steady hand by the time we catch up to him."

Sullivan scratched a spot below his right eye with his thumb.

"He hasn't used a gun in six months."

Brown, a better hand with a gun than Sullivan, said, "It ain't somethin' you forget how to do."

"A man can get rusty," Sullivan said.

"Think we'll need help?" Brown asked.

"Naw," Sullivan said, "the two of us is enough. Besides, we got the sheriff with us."

"And Mr. Delaware."

Sullivan snorted.

"All he's good for is money."

Brown raised his beer and said, "Here's to money."

"I'll drink to that." Sullivan clinked his mug against his partner's.

Chapter Twenty-nine

When Lancaster saw Big Bend, Kansas, ahead of them he stopped short.

"What's wrong?" Alicia asked.

"Nothing."

"Are we there yet?"

"Almost, honey," he said.

"Then why did we stop?"

"It's just been a long time since I've been here."

Six months that seemed like a lifetime. His shoulder still hurt sometimes where he took the bullet. Funny, he used to wish that bullet had killed him. These past few weeks he hadn't had that thought at all.

The thing that most surprised Lancaster about Alicia was how easily he was able to talk with her. He'd never been very comfortable with children, but he felt as if he'd known this little girl for a long time. Every time she craned her neck to look up at him, her blue eyes were filled with such trust that it amazed him. Invariably, he found himself looking away, because her eyes seemed ghostly to him, as if another little girl were regarding him through them.

"Is that where we're going?" she asked, pointing at Big Bend.

"That's it."

"Why aren't we moving?"

"Something bad happened the last time I was here."

"Then why did we come here?"

"Because," Lancaster said, "it's not right to run away from bad things."

"We're running away from my daddy," she said, "and he's bad."

"We're not really running away from him," Lancaster said. "It's more like we were running to here."

"And will something good happen now?"

"Yes," he said, sounding much surer than he felt, "something good will happen here."

He started walking his horse toward Big Bend, wondering how much time they had before Aaron Delaware caught up to them.

All through Oklahoma and part of Kansas he had started taking evasive action. Once, when he was walking the horse through a stream, he had to explain to Alicia it was to hide their tracks.

"Won't we still make tracks when we come out of the stream?" she asked.

"You're a smart little girl, have I ever told you that?"

She giggled, and pressed the back of her head against him.

"Lots of times."

He was getting used to that lump in the center of his chest when he was around her.

"Well, the answer to your question is yes, we will still make tracks."

"And won't they find them?"

"Yes."

"Then why are we doing it?"

"Because it will take more time to find them," he explained further, "and the more time and distance we can put between us and them, the better."

"Maybe they quit," she said hopefully. "Maybe they went home."

"I don't know about your father, Alicia," Lancaster said, "but Sheriff Mathis won't quit."

"Why not?"

"Because he's a good man."

"If he was a good man," she said wisely, "he'd leave us alone."

"I'm sure he wishes he could. . . ."

Chapter Thirty

Big Bend had changed very little since he was last there. As he rode down the main street the memory of what had happened there, right in front of the hotel, came rushing back to him, and he shuddered. He rode to the livery, dismounted, and lifted Alicia down.

Amazingly, as he helped her down from the horse, he felt more like himself than he had in six months. The night before, neither his hands nor his knees had shook, and he actually felt stronger than he had in a long time. He'd always liked riding the trail. It had been as if he drew sustenance from the land, and he guessed that this time was no different.

"Howdy," the liveryman said, coming out of the barn. "Can I help ya?"

After he was shot Lancaster had stayed in Big Bend just long enough to recover, and much of that time had been spent in the doctor's office. When he finally came out, though, he found that he was recognized on the street by quite a few people.

This man, however, did not seem to recognize him.

"Like to put our horse up."

"Sure thing. How long?"

"Couple of days."

"No problem. Take what you want off'n him and I'll take him inside. You can settle up when you leave."

Lancaster took his rifle, saddlebags, and the supply sack, which was the lightest it had ever been but had gotten them here with a few stops at small towns to refill it from time to time.

They walked to the hotel and registered, getting one room without an odd look from the clerk. It showed not everybody had a dirty mind.

When they were in the room Alicia sat on the bed and folded her hands in her lap.

"Is this where you're gonna leave me?"

She'd lost some of her eastern way of speaking after being on the trail with him for so long.

"What do you mean, leave you?"

"You ain't takin' me with you when you leave, are you?" It was more like an accusation than a question.

"Alicia, I brought you here to try and find a home for you."

"Why can't you find a home for both of us?"

"Because," he said, "I'm not fit to be your father, honey."

She turned her head and said, "Hmph, that's your opinion."

He went over and crouched in front of the bed.

"Don't be mad at me, Alicia," he said. "I'm trying to do the right thing by you."

She looked at him, then reached out and touched his face.

"You need a shave."

He took her with him to the barbershop. There he got a shave and a haircut, then they both went in the back and had a bath. Afterward he looked at himself in a mirror that hung on the wall of the bathhouse and saw how different he looked — much more like the old Lancaster. He still didn't feel like his old self, though. He didn't know if he ever would again. Two little girls had had such a profound effect on his life, and one of them he hadn't even known or spoken to.

"You look good, Lancaster," she said, sizing him up.

"So do you, Miss Alicia."

He took her hand, and they went in search of something to eat.

★ ★ ★

They had a hearty and hot supper, after which he bought her a piece of peach pie — it was her favorite — and himself a slice of apple. He paid for the meal, then took her hand and led her down the street.

"Why are we going in here?" Alicia asked.

"This is the sheriff's office," he explained. "The man inside is going to help us."

They walked to the door of the office, and Lancaster hesitated a moment before entering. Sheriff Kyle Thompson had told him never to come back to Big Bend, and there he was, six months later. He didn't know how the man was going to react. He remembered that even though the sheriff had run him out of town, he had been solicitous towards him because of what had happened.

He hoped the man would still feel that way.

When the door to his office opened Sheriff Kyle Thompson couldn't believe his eyes. The man looked the same, but curiously different at the same time. There was *something* different about him, but the sheriff couldn't put his finger on it.

"Lancaster."

"Hello, Sheriff."

The lawman gaped at him openly, then at the little girl.

"I thought I told you never to come back here."

"I know," Lancaster said, "but I didn't know where else to go."

"But . . . why come back here at all?" the lawman asked. "I'm surprised you weren't lynched in the street."

"It's pretty quiet out there."

"Why?" Thompson asked again, still stunned. "Why come back here?"

"This little girl needs help."

Thompson looked at Alicia, who was staring at him with wide, brown eyes.

"What kind of help does she need that you had to bring her here?"

"Can we sit and talk, Sheriff?" he asked. "It's a little bit of a story."

Still shocked at Lancaster's appearance back in Big Bend after six months, the man simply waved him to a chair. He watched in fascination as Lancaster sat and lifted the girl up onto his knee. She seemed very content to settle there, even happy. Six months earlier this man had killed a little girl much like this one — albeit accidentally — and now here he was, back in Big Bend, with another little girl. Thompson was glad

Lancaster had a story to tell, because he was still speechless.

"What the hell is this about?" he asked.

Lancaster told him.

Chapter Thirty-one

"That's quite a story," Sheriff Kyle Thompson said when he had all the facts. Almost all the facts. Lancaster left out the part about a posse being on his trail. After all, he didn't really know that for a dead-on fact, did he?

"It's all true."

"Yes," Alicia said, "it is." These were the first words she had spoken since they entered his office.

"I don't doubt that it is," Thompson said, speaking to both Lancaster and the little girl, "but it still doesn't explain why you came here."

"She needs a new home."

"Here?"

Lancaster nodded.

"With who?"

Lancaster stared at him. The sheriff seemed to have put on as much weight as Lancaster had taken off. His face was much fuller than Lancaster remembered, and it made him look older. Or maybe it was the disbelieving look on his face.

"Oh, no," Thompson said, "you can't be thinking . . ."

Lancaster nodded.

"Yes, I am."

"She'll never do it."

"I can ask her."

"She'll never agree to talk to you."

"You could ask her."

"That's what you want from me?" Thompson asked. "To act as a go-between?"

"Yes."

"Lancaster," the lawman said, "the woman has gone through hell these last six months and is tryin' to get her life back together."

"I realize that." He didn't bother telling the lawman that he'd been trying to do the same thing.

"She's even taken to working with some of the kids in town. We never had a school, you know, so she's started one —"

"Replaced her daughter with other children?"

"Not *replaced*," Thompson said. "She's just trying to . . . fill her days."

"Alicia could help her do that."

The sheriff looked exasperated.

"You could talk to her," Lancaster said. "She's a good woman."

"Yes, she is," Thompson said, "but this

may be too much to ask, even of a good woman."

"But you'll ask her?"

The sheriff remained silent, remembering all the times he'd seen Mary Pickens since the death of her daughter. Her eyes had been haunted things the first three months, seeming to sink into her head, with dark circles beneath them. During the fourth month she seemed to start coming out of it, some. By the fifth month her eyes did not always seemed haunted, and the dark shadows were fading. It was at that time she began to instruct a few of the younger children in town. At first some of the parents thought she was trying to use their children to replace her own, but they quickly realized that this was not the case. Mary Pickens simply had time on her hands, time that she was trying to put to good use.

"Sheriff?"

"Huh?"

"Will you ask her?"

"I'll talk to her, Lancaster . . ." Thompson said after a moment.

"Thank you."

"But you're gonna have to ask her . . . about Alicia."

"Me?"

"That's right."

"Sheriff," Lancaster said, his heart starting to beat faster, his palms starting to sweat, "I don't think I can do —"

"I'll approach her about talking to you," Thompson said, "seeing you, but after that I'm out of it, understand?"

"Sheriff —"

"Understand?"

Lancaster said after a moment, "Sure, I understand."

Chapter Thirty-two

"Why should I talk to him?" Mary Pickens demanded.

"To tell you the truth, Miz Pickens," the sheriff said, "I can't think of one single reason."

"He's got some nerve —"

"Except for the child," Thompson said.

"What child?"

"He has a child with him," Thompson said, "a little girl."

Mary Pickens hesitated, then in spite of herself asked, "How old?"

Thompson shrugged.

"Eight or nine, I guess."

Mary bit her lip.

"My daughter's age."

"Yes."

She hesitated again.

"What is *he* doing with a child?"

Sheriff Thompson told her the story.

Aaron Delaware and the rest waited patiently while Fred Brown examined the ground.

"What's wrong?" Delaware asked when Brown stood up.

"He's doubled back on us," Brown said. "He's been taking time to cover his tracks and lay false ones since Oklahoma and Kansas."

"Does that mean we've lost him?"

"No," the tracker said, "that just means he's not making it so easy."

He mounted up.

"Can you find his trail again?"

Brown looked at Delaware, then at Sullivan and the Sheriff.

"He'll find it," Sullivan said.

As they started forward again, Mathis leaned over to Sullivan.

"How many days behind him are we?"

"Two and a half, maybe three," Sullivan said. "With everything he's tried he's still only managed to gain another day on us. Don't worry, we'll catch him."

Mathis wasn't worried about catching up with Lancaster and the girl, he was just worried about what would happen when they did. Delaware, Brown, and Sullivan had been too quiet of late, speaking only when absolutely necessary. Mathis felt like the odd man out here, like everybody knew something he didn't.

He wondered when the other members of

his posse would show up, or if they had given up and gone back to Dunworthy.

"She said no."

Lancaster looked down at Alicia, who seemed totally uninterested.

"Actually," Thompson continued, "what she said was she didn't think she could do it. In fact, she acted the same way you did about seeing her."

"I can understand that."

"She's got more cause, don't you think?" Thompson asked.

"Yes, sir, I do. We'll be here a few days, Sheriff. Maybe she'll come around."

"Maybe."

They were in the lobby of the hotel, the one that was now called Kane House. Lancaster remembered being told that Hannibal Kane did not have the ego to put his name on a hotel. He guessed that had changed now.

"Hannibal Kane still a big man around here?" Lancaster asked.

"You ain't thinkin' about botherin' Mr. Kane, are you?" Thompson demanded.

"Why would I bother him?"

"That whole business with the man you killed, McCray," Thompson said. "You still say Kane was tryin' to hire you to kill him?"

"I never said that," Lancaster said, "McCray said that, right after he killed Carlyle and right before he tried to kill me."

"Mr. Kane, he said he didn't know anything about it. He said he never even talked to you."

"Well," Lancaster said, "I guess being rich and powerful don't necessarily keep you from being a liar, does it?"

"Don't start any trouble with Mr. Kane, Lancaster," the sheriff said.

"If he leaves me alone," Lancaster said, "I'll do likewise."

After the sheriff left, Lancaster and Alicia went for a walk. Six months seemed to have worked a miracle — hardly anyone appeared to recognize Lancaster. In fact, few people even looked at his face; they were too busy smiling at Alicia.

"Lancaster?"

"Yes."

"Did you kill somebody when you were here last time?"

"Yes, I did, honey."

"Who?"

"A man who tried to kill me."

"Did you get in trouble?"

"Not really."

"Is that the bad thing that happened

when you were here?"

"Part of it."

"What else is there?"

Lancaster hesitated, then decided that if he was going to persuade Mary Pickens to take Alicia in, he probably owed the child an explanation. She'd heard bits and pieces along the way, but he decided now to sit her down and tell her everything.

"Alicia, honey," he said, "let's go back to the hotel so we can talk."

Back in the room Lancaster explained the situation to Alicia as simply as possible, but she continued to amaze him with how intelligent she was and with her grasp on reality.

"You killed that other little girl by accident, Lancaster."

"Yes, I did."

"But her mother still might not be able to forgive you," the child said reasonably, " . . . not even if you give her me to replace her daughter."

"I'm not trying to replace her daughter," Lancaster said quickly — maybe a little too quickly.

"Then what are you doing?"

"I'm trying to help you, Alicia," he said. "I'm trying to fill a need that you have for a parent — a responsible parent who will raise you the right way."

"Not my father."

"No," Lancaster said, "not him."

"And not you?"

"If I could have a little girl of my own," he said, "I'd want her to be just like you, but —"

"But you *can* have me," Alicia said, as if that solved everything, "not a little girl *like* me . . . me!" She spread her arms when she said, "me!"

"I don't know the first thing about being a father, Alicia," he said. "I couldn't even buy you a dress, remember?"

"I don't care about that."

"I do," he said. "I care about it. You deserve a lot better than that."

She thought a moment, then said, "What about her father?"

"Whose father?"

"That other little girl?" Alicia asked. "Didn't she have a father?"

"No," Lancaster said, "her father is dead."

Alicia thought about that for a moment, then sighed and said, "I wish my father was dead."

"Alicia —"

"I do," she said. "If he was, we wouldn't have to be running, would we?"

"No," he said, "I suppose we wouldn't."

Chapter Thirty-three

"He's in my hotel?" Hannibal Kane demanded.

"Yes, sir," Sheriff Thompson said.

"What's he doing here?"

"Well, he's got a little girl with him and he's trying to find a home for her."

"Who would give him a little child after what he did to the Pickens girl?"

"I don't know."

"Are you sure he's not here for me?" Kane demanded. He stood up and went to his window, looking out nervously.

"Why would he be here for you?" Thompson asked.

Kane turned and looked at the lawman.

"Last time he was here didn't he tell lies about me?"

"I guess so . . . but what would bring him back?"

"Revenge."

"For what?" Thompson thought Kane was imagining things now. He didn't see any reason Lancaster would have for

194

wanting revenge on the man.

"I don't know," Kane said. "Who knows why madmen do what they do?"

"I don't think Lancaster is a mad—"

"Maybe he was hired to come here?" Kane asked, looking out the window again. "Did you ever think of that? Maybe somebody hired him to kill me."

"Why would he bring a little girl —"

"As a cover, man!" Kane said, whirling on the sheriff angrily. "I want you to run him out of town."

"He hasn't done anything —"

"This time!" Kane said. "What about last time?"

"That's over and done with."

"Not for Mary Pickens, it's not."

Thompson felt he was wasting his time here. Kane wasn't even letting him get a sentence out. He'd done his job by coming and informing Kane that Lancaster was in town.

"I have to go, Mr. Kane," Thompson said.

"And what about Lancaster?"

"I'll see what I can do."

Thompson turned and left while Kane stared after him in disgust. He watched out his window, and when he saw the sheriff hit the street he shouted, "Bailey!"

Mrs. Bailey came rushing in.

"Find Paxton for me."

"Now?"

He turned and said testily, "Yes, now! I want him right now!"

"Yes, sir!" she said, and withdrew.

Kane couldn't see his hotel from here, but knowing that Lancaster was there made him nervous and angry at the same time. He was nervous because he didn't know why the man had come back, and he was angry *because* he was nervous.

And afraid — and that made him madder than ever.

Frank Paxton knew the story about Lancaster, but he sat in a chair and let Hannibal Kane tell it to him all over again. It wasn't hard. Kane paid him enough to listen to the story ten times over.

"And now he's back," Kane finished. He was seated behind his desk with a glass of brandy. It had taken Mrs. Bailey a half hour to find Paxton and get him to Kane's office, and in that time Kane had had three brandies.

"Why?" Paxton asked.

"To get me, that's why! Why do you think?"

"Why does he want to get you?"

"I don't know!" Kane said, his voice shrill. "And I don't want to know. I just want him dead."

"And how do you suggest I do that?"

"Gun him down!"

"And will you keep the law off my back?"

"I won't have to," Kane said. "People remember what he did. No one will blame you for gunning him down in the street. Make it look like he started something. Do whatever you have to do, but kill him!"

"What about the little girl with him?"

"What about her?"

"Do you want her killed, too?"

Kane stared at Paxton. This was the man he'd found to work for him after Lancaster turned him down. Lancaster had killed McCray, but there were other men who had come for Hannibal Kane, and during the past six months Frank Paxton had taken care of all of them. Kane knew that Paxton would do anything for money — but it never occurred to him that he'd kill a child.

"Good God, no!" Kane said. "We don't need another dead child in this town. Just take care of Lancaster and don't worry about the child."

Paxton stood up and said, "Consider it done."

"Hire whatever help you need."

Paxton laughed.

"For a washed up gunhand like Lancaster? I won't need to hire any help."

"Fine," Kane said, shakily lifting the brandy snifter to his mouth, "just do it, then."

Paxton left the room, and Kane downed his brandy. The man never called him "sir," but that was the only complaint he had about Frank Paxton. He got the job done. Kane hoped he would continue to do that now.

Chapter Thirty-four

It was almost dark when they heard the horses.

"What's that?" Delaware asked. He stood up and took out his pistol. It was the first time Mathis knew that the man had a gun under his coat in a shoulder rig. He was going to have to pay more attention to the man as a danger, rather than simply as a wealthy blowhard.

"Put that away," Mathis said. "Those horses are behind us."

"Probably the rest of the posse," Sullivan said.

"Hello the fire!" a voice called out.

"Yep," Mathis said, "that's Eric Gates's voice. Come ahead!"

Slowly the three townsmen — Gates, Taggert, and Ford — rode in, looking bedraggled.

"Jesus Christ," Eric Gates complained, "I thought we'd never catch up to you."

"Well, step down and have some coffee and tell us what you found out."

The three men dismounted, tended to

their mounts first, then hunkered down by the fire with coffee and told their story.

They had followed the tracks of horses and wagons nearly to Arizona before they finally caught up and verified the fact that, while Lancaster's horse was with them, the man was not.

"That's what we figured," Sullivan said.

Gates looked at him.

"So if that's what everybody figured, why'd we have to bother?"

"We had to be sure, Eric," Mathis said, "that's all."

"So where are we headed now?" Gates asked.

"We're still following his trail," Fred Brown said.

"I've got an idea about that," Mathis said.

"What idea?" Sullivan asked.

"I think I know where he's going."

"What?" Delaware said. "Where?"

"Big Bend, Kansas."

"Why there?" Sullivan asked.

"Because that's where he had that trouble."

"What trouble?" Delaware demanded.

"He killed a little girl in Big Bend," Sullivan said.

"Jesus Christ!" Delaware exploded. "*Now* I find this out?"

"It was an accident," Mathis said. "She ran between him and another man during a gunfight. He's been trying to forget it ever since."

"So why's he goin' back there, Sheriff?" Brown asked.

"I think he needs to, to finally get rid of it," Mathis said.

"And what about Alicia?" Delaware asked.

Mathis shrugged.

"Maybe he figures that'd be as good a place as any to find her a home."

"She doesn't need a home," Aaron Delaware said. "She has a home, with me. We'd be there right now if that bitch of a mother hadn't taken her away from me."

Brown looked at Delaware.

"What?" Delaware asked.

"Nothin'."

"You got something on your mind?"

"I don't want to get fired."

"I won't fire you," Delaware said. "Go ahead, what are you thinking?"

Brown shrugged.

"I was just wonderin' what makes a woman up and leave a rich man and take their kid with them, that's all."

"Money isn't everything," Delaware said. "At least, that's what she thought."

"Why'd she leave, Delaware?"

"How do I know?" the man replied. "Maybe she didn't like getting hit."

"You hit her?" Mathis asked.

"Well, sure," Delaware said, "of course. I mean, all women need to be hit once in a while, just to keep them in line."

"I've killed a lot of men," Tom Sullivan said, staring across the fire at Aaron Delaware, "but I've never hit a woman."

"Me neither," Brown said.

"Come on . . . ," Delaware said in disbelief. He looked at Mathis. "You're a married man, Sheriff."

"Yes, I am."

"Don't tell me you've never had to slap your wife a bit to keep her in line."

"No," Mathis said, "I haven't had to do that, Mr. Delaware. See, I guess that's a big difference between back East and here in the West. See, out here we treat women with respect."

"I treat women with respect," Aaron Delaware said. "It's only my wife I ever hit."

There were a few moments of awkward silence before Mathis said, "Let's move on to something else. I figure if we head straight for Big Bend and don't stop, we can make up for lost time." He looked at Sullivan. "What do you think?"

Sullivan looked at Brown.

"I can keep tracking him," Brown said, "but you're right. If we do it your way, and he does go there, we make up a lot of time."

"That's it, then," Mathis said. "We'll head for Big Bend first thing in the morning. We should be there sometime tomorrow evening."

"And what if we get there and he's not there?" Delaware asked.

"Well, then I guess we'll just have to keep looking, Mr. Delaware," Sheriff Mathis said.

Chapter Thirty-five

The following day Sheriff Thompson had a visit from Mary Pickens. When she entered his office very early he was surprised to see her.

"Miz Pickens," he said, standing up, "good morning. I'd expect you to be at school about this time."

"I am on my way, Sheriff," she said. "I just came by to ask you to have that man Lancaster come by and see me after school."

"W-what?" He was stunned.

"I've decided to talk to him."

"But . . . why?"

She stared steadily into Thompson's eyes as she answered.

"Because I never have," she said. "I never saw him or spoke to him after . . . after what happened. I think I need to."

"Miz Pickens . . . are you sure?"

"No, Sheriff," she said, "I'm not sure. Just please have him come by my home at four o'clock this afternoon."

"Yes, ma'am," Thompson said. "I'll . . . I'll tell him."

"Thank you, Sheriff."

"Uh, ma'am?" he said as she headed for the door.

"Yes?"

"Do you want me to be there too?"

"That won't be necessary, Sheriff," Mary Pickens said. "I hardly think I'm in danger from the man, do you?"

"No, ma'am," he said. "I surely don't."

Lancaster was pleased when the sheriff brought him the news, but surprised, as well.

"What changed her mind?" he asked.

"I don't know," Thompson said. "She just marched into my office this morning and asked me to have you at her home at four o'clock."

"With Alicia?"

"Who?"

They were in Lancaster's hotel room, and he inclined his head toward Alicia, who was sitting on the bed.

Thompson frowned.

"She didn't say anything about the little girl."

"Well," Lancaster said, "I'll bring her. After all, that's why I'm here."

"I guess it'll be all right," Thompson said. "Just be there — and try not to upset her too much."

"I'll do my best."

Thompson opened the door to leave, then closed it again.

"What is it?" Lancaster asked.

"I don't know why I'm tellin' you this, but . . . I had to tell Kane you were in town."

"That's fine," Lancaster said. "I guess you thought that was part of your job. How did he take it?"

"Not well," Thompson said. "Not well at all, in fact. He was agitated . . . worse than agitated. He thinks you came here for him."

"For him?" Lancaster said. "Why?"

"I don't know," Thompson said, "but he's convinced. I . . . just wanted to tell you that."

"I'm obliged, Sheriff — for everything."

"There's gonna be trouble," Thompson said as he left the room, "I know it. . . ."

Obviously, Sheriff Thompson felt that Kane was going to send someone after him, and felt a responsibility to warn him. Now Kane knew about Lancaster, and Lancaster knew about Kane, and whatever happened happened. Lancaster didn't care, just as long as it happened after he placed Alicia in the care of Mary Pickens.

★ ★ ★

As Sheriff Thompson left the hotel he saw Frank Paxton leaning against the front of the building, rolling a cigarette.

"Mornin', Sheriff," Paxton said.

"Paxton."

"Gonna be some excitement in town?"

"What do you mean?"

"Mr. Kane told me about Lancaster," Paxton said. "Guess he's a little nervous, huh?"

"You listen to me, Paxton," Thompson said, turning to face the man. "Lancaster is here to talk to Mary Pickens, and that's all. Kane's got nothing to worry about."

Paxton licked the cigarette and said, "Mr. Kane likes to worry."

"I don't want any trouble, Paxton."

"Did you tell Lancaster that? Seems to me goin' to see the mother of the girl he killed is lookin' for trouble, don't you think?"

Paxton struck a match and lit the cigarette.

"There's not gonna be any trouble," Thompson said. "Miz Pickens asked to see Lancaster today at her house, at four. She's gonna see him willingly."

"Is that a fact?" Paxton replied. "Well, I'm glad you told me that, Sheriff. I'm mighty glad you told me."

"So there's not gonna be any trouble."

Paxton smiled and said, "There sure ain't gonna be any from me."

Chapter Thirty-six

Lancaster entered Mary Pickens's house nervously. He had never been so nervous before.

"This is a big house," Alicia said.

It was indeed a big house, two stories with several rooms on each floor. Six months earlier the sheriff had told Lancaster that Mary Pickens lost her husband a year before. He died leaving her the house, a lot of money — and their daughter.

"Yes, it is," Lancaster said.

Sheriff Thompson led them into the living room, where they waited, sitting side by side on the sofa. He went upstairs to get the lady of the house.

Moments later the sheriff came back down.

"She'll be along," he said. "I'll, uh, wait outside."

Before Lancaster could say anything, he was gone.

Lancaster watched Alicia, who was taking in her surroundings with great interest. He was looking at her eyes and wondered if something was wrong, when suddenly they heard someone coming down the steps.

Outside the house the sheriff sat in a chair on the porch and prepared to wait. He had no idea how this was going to go, but he was prepared — he thought — for anything. If Mary Pickens cried out for him, he was ready to rush in.

He was thinking so hard about what might happen that he didn't see the man slip up beside him. Before he knew it a gun slammed down onto his head and he slumped in the chair, unconscious.

Frank Paxton reversed the gun and slid it into his holster, then slipped his hands beneath the sheriff's arms and dragged him out of the chair and off the porch to the side of the house, out of the way.

Then it was Paxton who settled down to wait.

When Lancaster saw her his mouth went dry. He only remembered seeing her in the street that day, but he recognized her. She was walking stiffly down the stairs, staring at him. He swallowed and tried to keep himself from looking away.

"Mrs. Pickens —" he started, but she stopped him.

"Don't speak, please!" she said, harshly. He subsided, and the woman looked at Alicia for several moments before speaking. She walked to a soft cushioned chair and sat down.

"Come here, child."

Alicia looked at Lancaster, who nodded. The little girl got down from the sofa and walked over to stand in front of Mary Pickens. The woman looked at her with an entirely different expression.

"What's your name, child?"

"Alicia."

"What's your last name?"

Alicia shrugged.

"You don't know your last name?"

"It was Delaware," she said, "but my mommy told me that we changed it to Adams."

"Why did she change it?"

"So my father wouldn't find us."

"And why didn't she want your father to find you?"

"She said he was bad," Alicia said.

"In what way?"

"He used to hurt my mommy," she said. Lancaster was amazed at how level and strong her voice was while she was answering these questions. "He used to hit her."

"Did he ever hit you?"

"No," Alicia said, "but he would have if my mommy didn't take me away."

"Is that what your mother told you?"

Alicia nodded.

"And did you believe her?"

"Yes."

"Why?"

"Because my mommy didn't lie to me."

"Ever?"

"Ever."

"Alicia," Mary Pickens said, "are you afraid of your father?"

"Yes."

"Why?"

"Because he sent a man to kill my mommy."

Lancaster couldn't see Alicia's face, but it was either something there or something in what she said that caused Mary Pickens's face to dissolve in tears.

"Oh, honey," she said, and took the little girl into her arms. When Lancaster realized that they were both crying, he knew he had made the right decision.

He waited.

Mary and Alicia cried for a while, with the woman stopping first. Lancaster thought that the little girl had probably needed this for a long time. He also noticed that Mary

Pickens never looked at him over the little girl's shoulder. In fact, she had not looked at him since she first came down. That was why he was surprised when she finally did.

"You want me to keep this child?"

"Yes," he said. "She needs a home."

Mary held Alicia at arm's length as the child's sobs subsided.

"Alicia, would you like to stay here?"

The child snuffled, then answered.

"Can Lancaster stay, too?"

Mary Pickens looked shocked.

"Why would you want him to stay?"

"He saved my life."

Mary hesitated, then said, "I see."

"I can't stay, honey," Lancaster said to Alicia. "You know that. We talked about it."

Alicia hung her head and said, "I know," in a very small voice.

Mary Pickens looked at Lancaster again, then at Alicia.

"Do you know that I had a little girl your age?"

"Yes, ma'am."

"And that this man killed her?"

Alicia nodded, then said, "It was an accident, though."

"Yes," Mary Pickens said, "yes, I suppose it was."

For a few moments she stared into space, at something only she could see. Whatever she saw, though, seemed to change her in that moment, and when she looked at Alicia again it was with a different mind-set. Lancaster had been sure that she was going to take the child, but suddenly he knew she was not.

"I'm sorry," she said, shaking her head and backing away from Alicia. She didn't move back physically, but suddenly she seemed to have. Again she said, "I'm sorry" to Alicia. "I can't do this."

"That's all right," Alicia said. She walked back to where Lancaster was sitting and surprised him by putting an arm around his shoulder. "I want to stay with Lancaster anyway."

"Honey —" he started, but Mary Pickens cut him off.

"I don't know how you could have instilled such . . . such loyalty into this child."

Lancaster didn't know what to say to that.

"Please leave my house," Mary Pickens said, then rose and walked back to the stairs.

"Come on, Alicia." Lancaster took her hand, and they headed for the front door.

Chapter Thirty-seven

When they stepped out onto the porch Lancaster immediately knew something was wrong.

"Are we leaving?" Alicia asked.

Lancaster looked around. The sheriff had said he would be waiting outside, and yet he wasn't there. He had struck Lancaster as being concerned about how this meeting went. He didn't think the lawman would have simply left.

Not willingly.

Then he saw the man in front of the house. He was standing with his hands clasped in front of him, his weight more on one leg than the other. He wore a gun on his left hip, and he looked to Lancaster like a man who knew how to use it. At that moment he could have been twenty or forty. His age did not matter to Lancaster, so his conscious mind did not even hazard a guess.

"I'm Paxton," the man announced. "Frank Paxton. Do you recognize my name?"

The name was vaguely familiar.

"I think I've heard it."

The man laughed.

"You think?"

"Once," Lancaster said, "maybe twice."

"You're Lancaster, right?"

"That's right."

Paxton raised his right hand, scratched his cheek, then returned it to where it had been at his belt.

"I've heard *your* name," he said. "I'd heard it even before I came to this town, but a lot more since I've been here. You have a reputation in this town."

"Do I?"

"Yes," Paxton said, "you do . . . as a baby killer."

Lancaster felt his face flush. He suddenly knew there was no way out of this. He hadn't faced another man with a gun in six months, and the last time had changed his life forever.

"How do you like the sound of that?" Paxton asked. "Baby killer?"

Lancaster didn't answer.

"No," Paxton said, "I didn't think you would like it, but what are you gonna do? That's how the people of this town think of you."

"They've got the right to think anything they want," Lancaster said.

"Baby killer," Paxton said again, "and here you are, botherin' the woman whose baby you killed."

"We weren't bothering anybody," Alicia said, defiantly.

Without looking at her Paxton snapped, "You shut up, girl! I ain't talkin' to you."

"Quiet, Alicia," Lancaster said. He had felt her start when the man yelled, and he was now trying to think of a way to get her out of the line of fire.

"I'm talkin' to the baby killer, here!" Paxton shouted.

"What'd you do with the sheriff?" Lancaster asked.

"He's takin' a little siesta," Paxton said. "By the time he wakes up it'll be too late for him to do anything."

"He'll be able to do one thing," Lancaster said.

"What's that?"

"Arrange for your burial."

Paxton laughed.

"I heard you fell into a bottle, Baby Killer," Paxton said. "Fell in and couldn't crawl out. That right?"

"For a while."

"Oh, not anymore?"

"No."

"Well, good for you," Paxton said. "You

sobered up just in time to die."

"Let the child walk away," Lancaster said.

Paxton looked pained.

"I'm not gonna shoot her," he said. "Oh, I see, but you might, huh? You gonna kill another baby?"

"Just let her walk away, Paxton. This is between you and me . . . and Kane, I suppose. You are being paid by Kane, aren't you?"

Paxton didn't answer.

"But he's paying you for me, not the girl," Lancaster went on. "Let the child walk away."

"Don't worry about her," Paxton said, dropping his hands from his belt so they hung at his sides, "worry about yourself. It's time to die, Lancaster."

"Alicia," Lancaster said, "get behind —"

He didn't have a chance to finish. Behind him the door of the house slammed open and Mary Pickens came running out shouting, "No! Nooooo! You're not going to kill another one. I won't allow it!"

She grabbed Alicia in her arms and lifted her off the ground and away from Lancaster.

"You can kill each other if you want," she said, "but I will not watch another innocent child die!"

"Take her, then," Paxton snapped, "and get out of the way, you stupid cow."

Mary Pickens favored each man with the same look of pure hatred, then turned and ran into the house with Alicia, slamming the door behind her.

Lancaster heard Alicia calling his name as the door banged shut.

Chapter Thirty-eight

"Well, there now," Paxton said. "Now the little girl's safe. You ready to die, Baby Killer?"

"If you'd asked me that question at any time during the past six months — up to a few weeks ago — I would have said yes."

"And now?"

"And now I'm ready to live again, Paxton," Lancaster said, "and that's bad news for you."

Paxton frowned, because suddenly Lancaster looked different. He couldn't quite put his finger on what it was. Could it have been the removal of the little girl from harm's way? Whatever it was, Paxton didn't like it.

"Come on, Paxton," Lancaster said, "I've got to get on with the rest of my life, and you're blocking the way."

Maybe, Paxton thought, maybe I should have brought help, like Kane said.

There were two shots. When she heard

them from inside the house Alicia began to scream Lancaster's name, and fought to get away from Mary Pickens.

Mary, shocked and amazed by the child's resolve and strength, could not hold her. Alicia broke free and ran for the door.

"Alicia! No!"

Just for a moment — a split second — she had almost called Alicia "Becky," but her Becky was dead, and this child was alive, and she desperately needed to keep her that way.

She ran after Alicia, who burst through the front door and outside. As Mary Pickens went through the door she saw Alicia clinging to the leg of Lancaster, who was standing over the fallen body of Paxton.

She heard a groan then, and looked to her left. She saw Sheriff Thompson, hatless and bleeding from the head, stagger into sight from the side of the house. She rushed to help him, but as she did she heard Alicia's voice.

"Lancaster, Lancaster," Alicia said, almost chanting, "Lancaster, you're all right, you're all right . . ."

"Alicia," he said, "you can call me . . . Will."

Chapter Thirty-nine

When Lancaster burst into Hannibal Kane's office Mrs. Bailey stood up and held her hands out in front of her.

"You can't —" she started, but she had no time to finish.

"Get out of my way," Lancaster commanded, and swept her aside with his arm.

He slammed Kane's door open and the man looked up from his desk, startled at first and then, when he saw who it was, frightened. He grabbed for his desk drawer, where he kept a gun, but he was too slow. Lancaster was on him before he could get it open.

Lancaster dragged him out of his chair and slapped him three times very quickly, three stinging, jarring blows. The third blow split Kane's lip, and blood dripped down his chin.

Lancaster pulled him close so that their noses almost touched.

"I should throw you out this window, you old fool!" he shouted.

"Wait — please — you can't —" Kane stammered.

Lancaster slapped him one more time, then threw him back into his chair. It started to tip backward, but Lancaster grabbed it, righted it, and got into Kane's face once again. The man's eyes were wide with fright, and his head was still swimming from the blows.

"If I wanted to kill you I could do it right now," he said. "Do you understand me?"

"Y-y-yes," Kane stuttered.

"Your man Paxton wasn't good enough," Lancaster said. "He's dead. If you send another man after me I'll kill that one, and then I will come here and kill you. Do you understand that?"

"Y-y-yes, I u-understand." Blood dripped from his lip onto his expensive white shirt.

"As far as I'm concerned, Kane," Lancaster said, "we're finished. We have no reason to ever see or talk to each other again."

"Y-y-yes."

"The sheriff might have different intentions," Lancaster went on. "Your man attacked him, and I don't think he's too happy with you."

Lancaster walked to the door, then turned back to Kane.

"If you want to go for that gun in your desk, I'll give you the chance now."

"N-n-no!" Kane said, throwing up his hands. "No, no, no, we're through."

"Just make sure you remember that."

He left the office and went past a frightened Mrs. Bailey.

"If I was you," he said to her without stopping, "I'd find a new job."

He walked out and slammed the door behind him.

When he got to the doctor's office, the sheriff's head was bandaged and the doctor was giving him instructions.

"You'll need some rest," the physician said to him.

"Yes, yes, I know," Thompson said.

He was in the act of putting his shirt on, but he paused when Lancaster entered.

"Did you kill him?" he demanded. "I hope you didn't kill him."

"I didn't," Lancaster said. "He's all yours."

"What did you do to him?"

"I slapped him and threatened to throw him out the window. I made it clear that I could have killed him if I wanted to."

"And? How did he take it?"

"Who knows?" Lancaster said. "He's

224

bloodied and bowed now, but who knows what he'll do when he has time to think about it."

"He'll have time to think if I have anything to say about it," Thompson said. "Letting him walk all over me is one thing, but letting him get away with sending his man to club me, and putting that little girl's life in danger . . . Say, where is she?"

"Mrs. Pickens has her."

Thompson looked surprised.

"Is she going to keep her?"

"She said no, but she's got her now. I think maybe she wants to get acquainted. I figure to leave them alone for a few hours."

"Maybe you want to freshen up and get something to eat?"

"Maybe. . . ."

"What's wrong?"

Lancaster looked at Thompson.

"You ever feel like somebody just walked on your grave?"

"No," the lawman said, "and I hope I never do. Come on. I better stay with you, in case somebody tries to give you some trouble."

"You're supposed to be resting," the doctor said.

"Yeah, yeah, Doc," Thompson said. He tried to put his hat on, then winced and held it in his hand. "Send me a bill."

Chapter Forty

"That's Big Bend," Fred Brown announced.

"I should have thought of this earlier," Sheriff Mathis said, "instead of spending all that time trying to root out his sign."

"He was good," Brown said, "but I would have found him eventually."

"Well, maybe we have already," Gates said. "I hope so. I'd like this to be the end of the trail, huh, boys?"

Ford and Taggert nodded.

"My wife ain't so good at running my business," Ford said. "I got to get back."

"Maybe you should have smacked her around a little, Ben," Taggert said. "That seemed to work for Mr. Delaware."

"Oh yeah?" Ford asked. "Then why are we here?"

"Idiots," Delaware muttered. These men, these small-town shopkeepers, were not worthy of his time or his anger.

"Why would he come back here?" Delaware asked, speaking aloud to anyone who cared to answer. "It's idiotic."

"I don't know," Mathis said. "It's probably the last place he figured we'd look."

"Why don't we go and ask him?" Sullivan said, and started his horse forward. The others followed.

"Sheriff," Lancaster said.

"What?"

Lancaster put his hand on the man's arm and pointed with his chin. Thompson looked and saw seven men riding toward them from the other end of town.

"Something you forgot to tell me?"

"It's a posse, from Dunworthy, Texas."

"How do you know?"

"That's Sheriff Mathis, and one of those men is Aaron Delaware, Alicia's father."

"Her father? What's he doin' with the posse?"

"He wants back what's his. I guess he decided to come along."

"Why would the sheriff allow that?"

"Somehow," Lancaster said, "I don't think he's got much choice."

"Why not?"

"Aaron Delaware is a rich man, Sheriff. You know how rich men get their way, don't you?"

"I have firsthand knowledge of that," Thompson said, "as you well know." He looked down the street. "Quite a coincidence, them ridin' in here right now, don't you think?"

"I could have used another day," Lancaster said. "I guess I didn't shake them as well as I thought. I better go talk to them."

"I'll go with you," Thompson said, "in case they try to give you some trouble."

"Who are they?" Delaware asked as they approached two men who were on foot. One of them was hatless, with a bandage on his head. "Is that Lancaster?"

"One of them is wearing a badge," Sullivan said, speaking to Fred Brown.

"The local law," Mathis said. "He's going to want an explanation."

"Is that Lancaster?" Delaware asked again.

"That's him," Mathis said.

"Where the hell is my little girl?"

The two men on foot and the seven on horseback stopped within twenty feet of each other.

"I'm Sheriff Thompson."

"Sheriff Mathis, from Dunworthy, Texas," the other lawman replied.

"You're a little far afield, Sheriff," Thompson said. "What can I do for you?"

"We're lookin' for this man," Mathis said, nodding at Lancaster.

"Goddammit," Aaron Delaware said, "where's my daughter?"

Lancaster looked at the man.

"She's safe."

"Where?"

"Away from you."

"You think we won't find her?"

"Take it easy —" Mathis started, but Delaware was not to be denied.

"I want to see her — now."

Lancaster shook his head.

"She doesn't want to see you."

"What are you talking about?" Delaware demanded. "She's my daughter. Why wouldn't she want to see me?"

"Because you had her mother killed," Lancaster said, "and she knows it."

Delaware looked around nervously, then decided to bluster it out.

"That's preposterous! She'd never believe such a thing."

"How do you know that, Lancaster?" Mathis asked.

Lancaster answered while keeping his eyes on the two men to Delaware's right. If there was going to be trouble, it would come from them. The others were members of the posse, but they were townspeople, merchants. These two were professionals.

"The little girl told me."

"She's . . ." Delaware started.

"What?" Lancaster asked. "Crazy?"

"Mistaken."

"I don't think so."

"Her mother turned her against me."

"She heard it," Lancaster said. "She heard Josiah Alton say he worked for you, just before he killed her mother . . . your wife. What kind of a man does that, Delaware?"

Now Delaware looked to the two lawmen.

"This man's a kidnapper," he said. "Somebody arrest him."

The two sheriffs exchanged a glance.

"Maybe," Mathis said, "we should talk to the little girl."

"There's nothing to talk to her about!" Aaron Delaware said. "Christ, she's only . . . six or seven."

"She's eight, Delaware," Lancaster said. "You don't know how old your own daughter is?"

"Seven, eight, what the hell is the difference? She's mine. Nobody takes what's mine." He looked to the lawmen again, and at the posse members. "Aren't you going to do something?"

"I think talking to the little girl would be a good idea," Sheriff Thompson said.

It had never occurred to Aaron Delaware that his own daughter might speak against him, that she might have been present when Josiah Alton killed his wife.

He turned and looked at Brown and Sullivan.

"Take him!" he said.

The two men hesitated.

"Do what I'm paying you to do!"

"You paid us to find him," Tom Sullivan said, "not to gun him down in front of two lawmen."

"It would be a fair fight," Delaware said. "Isn't there some kind of code of the West? A fair fight?"

"One man against one man, Mr. Delaware," Lancaster said, "that's a fair fight."

Delaware looked directly at Brown.

"You take him, man to man."

"Take him yourself." Even Fred Brown couldn't abide a man who would have his own wife killed in front of his daughter. Besides, he already had plenty of Delaware's money in his pockets.

Delaware looked at Sullivan.

"How about you? I'll double what I paid you."

Sullivan spat before he said, "I ain't working for a man who had his own woman killed."

"But I already paid you a lot of money!"

"And we earned it," Sullivan said. "We're through now."

"You do it yourself, Delaware," Lancaster said.

"That's ridiculous," Delaware said. "I — I don't have a gun."

"Here," Brown said, unbuckling his gunbelt and holding it out to Delaware, "use mine."

The two men stared at each other for a few moments, Aaron Delaware perspiring heavily and biting his lip.

"Take it!" Lancaster ordered.

Chapter Forty-one

They had attracted an audience, people stopping on both sides of the street to watch what was transpiring. It grew very quiet as they all waited for Aaron Delaware to make up his mind.

"Wait, wait, wait," Delaware finally shouted, putting his hands up. "Don't shoot. Never mind. I don't have to have her. You can keep her."

"But she's your daughter," Mathis said. "You rode all this way looking for her. You hired these two men, paid them handsomely. You're ready to give her up after all that?"

"I don't want her bad enough to die for her," Delaware said, scowling. "I'm a businessman. I know when to cut my losses."

Everyone — Lancaster, the lawmen, the posse, the spectators — stared at Aaron Delaware with disgust.

"Okay," Delaware shouted, "so I won't win a blue ribbon for being a great father!"

"Too bad for Alicia." Lancaster put his

hands behind him so no one would see they were shaking. He'd already killed one man today, and he wasn't sure he had anything left in him for another gunfight. It had been a long time. . . .

"That's enough," Sheriff Mathis said, putting himself and his horse between Lancaster and Delaware. "Keep your gun, Brown."

The man strapped it back on.

"You two been paid?" Mathis asked.

"Up to now," Sullivan said.

"I think that's all you're gonna get," Mathis said. "Sheriff Thompson?"

The sheriff of Big Bend stepped forward and said to Brown and Sullivan, "I suggest you fellas ride out. I wouldn't want you to change your minds about working for this man."

Sullivan stared at the sheriff, then looked at Lancaster, nodded, and turned his horse.

"You're pretty good," Brown said to Lancaster, "but I found you."

"Yeah," Lancaster said, "you did."

Brown turned his horse and rode after Sullivan.

"Sheriff," Mathis said, "I'd like to freshen up a bit and then talk to the little girl."

"You and your men are welcome to rooms at the hotel, Sheriff."

Mathis turned and told his men they were done.

"Head home or get a room — it's your choice."

The three men decided to get rooms, get some rest, and head back the next day. They rode on to deposit their horses at the livery, leaving the two lawmen, Aaron Delaware, and Lancaster on the street.

Delaware glared at the two sheriffs and said, "You're siding with a kidnapper."

"Mr. Delaware," Mathis said, "if I could have proved that Alton worked for you back in Dunworthy, you wouldn't have gotten this far."

"But —"

"I don't hold with men who have women killed," Thompson said, "especially their child's mother."

"You wanna show me where the little one is?" Mathis asked Thompson.

"I'd be happy to," the sheriff of Big Bend said. "What about Lancaster?"

Mathis looked at Lancaster as if this were a man he had never seen before. Sober, clean, he'd put some weight back on; this was an entirely different man. You could see it in his eyes.

"I don't think I need him anymore," he said. "Lancaster, you plannin' on comin' back to Dunworthy anytime soon?"

Lancaster looked at Mathis and said, "I doubt it."

"You need him?" Mathis asked Thompson.

"I guess not." He looked at Lancaster. "You're not stayin' in town, are you?"

"Just long enough to finish my . . . business with Mrs. Pickens."

"Good," Thompson said. "You done this little girl a good turn, Lancaster, but I still don't think I want you in my town."

"I'll be on my way," Lancaster said, "as soon as I'm sure the girl is safe."

"Oh, I get it," Delaware said. "Trying to trade my daughter for the girl you killed? Trying to ease your guilt, Lancaster?"

Lancaster looked at Delaware. If Sheriff Mathis hadn't moved between them, Lancaster might have killed him then and there. Delaware's words hurt more, for some reason, than having Frank Paxton call him a baby killer.

"Shut up, Delaware," Mathis said.

"Follow me, Sheriff," Thompson said, and the three men moved away, leaving Lancaster standing in the street alone.

Epilogue

The first thing he noticed about Alicia when he saw her again was that she had brown eyes. How odd. Why had he thought she had blue eyes this whole time?

Was he crazy?

Maybe he had been. Maybe that had been the problem.

"Are you leaving?" Alicia asked.

"Yes, honey."

"I wish you weren't."

"I have to," he said. "It wouldn't be right."

"I know," she said. "You told me."

"Miz Pickens will take good care of you."

"She's nice."

They were standing on the front porch of Mary Pickens's house. Sheriffs Mathis and Thompson had already been there with Aaron Delaware, but they hadn't allowed Delaware to see his daughter. They had talked with Alicia, then asked her if she wanted to see her father. She had said no. She'd recounted all of this to Lancaster.

"I never want to see him again."

Lancaster had the feeling that would change when she got older. He wondered what the two lawmen would decide to do with Aaron Delaware. He really didn't care, though, as long as Alicia was safe. He intended to ride right from the Pickens house out of town.

"I don't blame you, honey."

"Lancaster?"

"Yeah?"

"Can I kiss you goodbye?"

"Sure you can."

He squatted down, and she gave him a hug and a kiss on the cheek. He looked into her eyes again, just to make sure. Yep. They were brown.

"What's wrong?" she asked.

"You have beautiful brown eyes."

"Thank you. Will you come and see me?"

"Sure I will, Alicia."

She hugged him tightly again and said into his ear, "You probably won't."

"Goodbye, sweetie."

He stood up.

"Goodbye . . . Will."

He waited until she went into the house without looking back at him, then walked to his horse and mounted up. That lump in his chest seemed to have grown huge, and he wondered how long it would take for it to go away.

He wondered, also, what would happen that night when he camped and went to sleep.

He wondered if he'd seen the last of the ghost with blue eyes.